The Current

Meagan Kish

ISBN: 978-1-943789-97-9

Copyright 2018

Taylor and Seale Publishing, LLC
Daytona Beach, Fl.
taylorandseale.com
386-760-8987
386-481-5020
mk@taylorandseale   386-760-8987

Our books are found on Amazon,
Barnes and Noble and Books a Million
For special prices on large orders, contact
mk@taylorandseale

Dedication

For my girls—
May you soar on wings like eagles.
Isaiah 40:30-31

Acknowledgments

So many thanks must be given to my family, friends, teachers and professors who have gotten me to this point.

To my husband, Dan—I love you more than I could ever express in words. Thank you for being my partner in this life.

To my family—thank you for supporting me and not laughing me out of the door when I announced I would be getting an English degree! Thank you especially to Mom and Grammy who endured and provided feedback on the many drafts of this work over the years.

To my friends—thank you for your encouragement throughout this process and for not retreating from the room when I launched into unsolicited history lessons on the happenings of the 1890's South.

For my teachers and professors who instilled an appreciation for the classics and the basics of a good novel, thank you.

To my editor, Dr. Melissa Doerrfeld—you took my mess and made it readable and brought such a poignant knowledge of Southern literature to this work. Thank you so much.

Finally, to my agent Charlene Visco—you took a chance on a nobody and stuck with me through every step. I am forever grateful to you.

Chapter 1

Moon Springs, Georgia
February, 1893

The sharp piercing of twigs snapping under her bare feet mattered little as she raced towards the riverbank. Mother would scold her for catching her skirt on that fallen log dozens of yards back, but she didn't care. She didn't even hesitate when she got to the river's edge and plunged beneath its icy surface. Flipping to her back, she spread her arms and surrendered her body to the current. Her hands and feet numbed from winter's last grip on the water, but she didn't mind. She gazed up at the pitch-black sky shrouded in clouds and listened to the gentle rustle of the water as she traveled towards the river docks in town. It was surprisingly relaxing—the feeling of the freezing water seeping into her pores, the swelling pile of thick auburn hair kneading the back of her neck.

Ghostly images of souls who had drowned in this same river through the years flashed in her memory, but again, she wasn't deterred. At nineteen, she was built more like a farmhand than the dainty young lady her mother wished her to be, and she could out-swim a salmon. At least that's what her father said.

1

And that's why she was here, now, in the frigid water on a cold winter night. She needed to think clearly and could only do that when the unwelcome emotions that were tyrannizing her thoughts were frozen out by the black waters. Only when she was completely alone in the natural surroundings of the river, *her river,* whose bends and rapids she knew like the back of her hand, could she think reasonably.

Ethan had betrayed her—and it had nothing to do with the fact that he'd lost everything when the railroad failed. Of course the rest of the town was horrified that their favorite son, who'd carried so much potential when he left for the gleaming promises of Savannah's burgeoning railroad industry, had squandered away everything in a matter of months. The railroad he'd promised would change everything had never arrived. Oak County's oldest banking family had lost what had taken more than a century to build in a matter of months, all at the hands of Amelia's fiancé. But that made absolutely no difference to her. The money meant nothing. Her parents had plenty and would offer Ethan a job with Sullivan's Mercantile until he was back on his feet. She didn't even worry about the social implications of wedding a ruined man. She'd marry him anyway in a heartbeat. The money, the reputation, it was all meaningless to her.

What grieved her was his deceitfulness about the whole thing.

She could sense that Ethan had been holding back from her the minute he'd returned. After greeting him at the carriage station, she'd given him a day to decompress before visiting him at his family estate.

2

The next afternoon, she had approached the stately wrought iron gate of Morrow House swiftly with determination, rehearsing the exact thing she intended to say to show her unwavering support. "Everything will be just fine. There is always a job for you running the mercantile, and I'd be happy to work alongside you." All things any well-bred woman worth her salt would say. She knew what she had to do and who she had to be, for him.

What she hadn't anticipated was the delusional stranger who greeted her as she came into the parlor.

As she was escorted into the pristinely decorated room, covered from floor to ceiling in the finest green silks and gold-threaded tapestry fabrics, Ethan nearly catapulted out from behind the imposing dark walnut Davenport.

"Millie, what timing!"

"I was just thinking about how wonderful it feels to be back home, and that the only thing that would top off this marvelous day would be if I could see you, and here you are!"

Rubbing her strained shoulder that he'd nearly dislocated when he whirled her around the floor, Amelia suspiciously peered up at his slightly crooked yet markedly handsome smile. He seemed so whimsical and disconnected from reality, it was alarming.

"Ethan, are you ill?"

"Of course not. Why do you ask?"

"Well, you seem..." she searched for the right words, remembering her mission to bolster his confidence, "Not that it matters to me, of course, but, you've just come home from all the…challenges…you

3

met with in Savannah, and I'm just wondering if maybe you need some more rest."

His eyes left hers for just a moment, but one certainly not lost on her, then he looked back and smiled, "That's nothing. I don't want to hear another word about it. Come, sit down and tell me all about the wedding plans."

"Now I know you're ill," she laughed, "because I've never met a man in my life with an ounce of interest in planning a wedding." She sat down on the edge of the velvet chaise opposite his, her smile disappearing as quickly as it had come. "But in all seriousness, Ethan, I am the last person to be concerned with your family fortune, and you know that I would marry you tomorrow with nothing but the clothes on your back, but I do think you ought to take this all a bit more seriously. It has affected so many people in such a tremendous way. Think of poor May. She was inconsolable when we got your letter. She's so worried about you."

Ethan's twin sister, May, who was married to Amelia's older brother, Samuel, was expecting their first child in a few months and was so fragile to begin with. She was a marvelous sister and friend, but she had absolutely no stamina. Children can get into so much mischief, Amelia wondered what unwelcome adventures motherhood would bring to her if her baby had even a fraction of the Sullivan spirit. She couldn't even count how many scrapes and bruises she and Samuel and their younger sister, Adele, had come home with throughout the years.

Ethan feigned shock, "It wounds me that you think I'm not over the moon about the wedding. Actually, I was hoping you would throw in a detail or two about that stunning dress your mother ordered from her designer in Paris. I would love something to picture while I lie in bed during these next days, waiting for the night when you can finally be there with me."

Amelia's cheeks grew hot as he crossed the room to pull her to her feet.

"I've missed you," he whispered as he bent to kiss her softly.

"I've missed you, too."

She felt so safe in his arms, it took her a moment to remember why she'd come in the first place. She unfolded herself and stepped back, looking up at him with as stern a face as she could muster.

"Ethan, please. We do actually need to figure out a few things."

"Such as?"

"Well, firstly, have you written to your friend in Charleston to tell him that we won't be coming there on our honeymoon?"

"Why? Have you changed your mind as to where you'd like to go?"

"No, of course not. I just know we can no longer afford it. I don't think it would be wise to use the little money you have left on something as frivolous as travel when it should probably be utilized to update our new house instead."

Ethan had recently purchased a charming three -bedroom stone cottage at the edge of town. Amelia was eager to put her own touch on it, as it had previously been inhabited by a widowed doctor who had passed away. It had great potential to be a lovely home, but in its current state more closely resembled a cave with its dim walls and the pervading odor of decades of pipe tobacco smoke.

Now it was Ethan's turn to frown. He crossed his arms, exasperated. "Really, it is not as bad as all that, Amelia. This whole thing has been blown completely out of proportion by those nosy gossips like your mother who have nothing better to do than wag their tongues and turn you against me in the process."

"Insulting my mother is completely unnecessary. Besides, I don't see what you mean. You left with money, invested it, and instead of making more, came back with much less. Those are simply the facts. How can it be described any other way? I don't need to be a banker to know that the money for an extravagant and unnecessary honeymoon just isn't there. What am I blowing out of proportion?"

"Everything!" he growled. "Me, Savannah— my family's money. Everyone in this town seems to think that I have come home bankrupt with nothing more to do than hole up with you in an abandoned cottage and beg for your father to rescue me. I have plenty of money left, I didn't lose everything, and frankly, it's none of their business even if I had. I don't owe those people anything! That's just business. Besides, it wasn't just me you know. The entire country is falling to ruin, yet somehow I'm the only one the state of Georgia cares to mention."

"I'm sorry." She stepped cautiously towards him as one approaches a wounded animal and slowly

6

put her hand on his forearm. He flinched and looked away. "You're hardly the only victim of these times. I'm not accusing you of being a bad businessman, Ethan. I trust your economic sense implicitly. I'm just trying to help. Let me do that, because in a few weeks, your problems will be mine. I have been talking to Father, and he's been talking of retiring soon. You and I could run the mercantile together. I could manage the store, and you could run the business side."

"That's ridiculous. You're not going to work in the store. Tell your father thank you, but no. In fact, I'll tell him myself. There's no reason for you to be involved."

She knew he was trying to sound heroic, but his demeaning opinion of her capabilities to contribute to their future family infuriated her. But she had better sense than argue that point now.

She took another calming breath and replied, "Ethan, Moon Springs is a small place, and I just think it will take time for the people here to trust you with their money again. I'm just trying to prepare for the inevitable struggle we will face when we are married."

He stared through the drawn curtains down the lane towards town for a moment. Then, dropping his defensively hunched shoulders, he stepped towards her. His thick brown hair fell in front of his eyes as he looked down at her and cupped her face with his hands.

"I'm sorry, Millie. I shouldn't have yelled at you. I just wish everyone would stop assuming that I'm a ruined man. I promise you. I've handled everything. You've nothing to worry about, trust me."

"Of course I do."

And for a few glorious days, it seemed as if it really would all blow over.

But that feeling was swept far downstream with the current now as Amelia slowly trudged out of the river, dragging her heavily soiled dress behind her. She skillfully scaled the nearly vertical embankment without slipping and began the trek back towards Sullivan's Pine, her family's farm, nestled half a mile outside of town. Seeing the lights of the village softly glowing through the trees, she realized she had drifted a rather long distance from where she had entered the water but welcomed the long walk back home. An owl hooted in the tree just above her head as she forged her own path through the enormous and fragrant Georgia pines instead of taking the long way via the road. She inhaled deeply. She felt more at home here, among the scents and sounds of the forest, than she ever did within the walls of the mansion where she lived with her parents and sister.

As she passed the gate to Ethan's family home, Morrow House, she paused and recalled earlier that evening when she had overheard Ethan arguing with his brother, Bennett, after her family had dined with the Bennigans. She could tell throughout the dinner that Bennett was upset about something when his usual mischievous tone was lacking any warmth or charm, but he didn't give any indication as to what troubled him. A bit later, when they were all enjoying coffee and tea in the drawing room, Adele realized she'd lost her new apricot chiffon scarf. Ethan offered to return to the dining room to look while the others searched the other rooms. When their father found it under a chair in the foyer, Amelia went to tell Ethan, but she found the dining room empty. Curious, she continued on down the hall but paused when she heard hushed voices coming out of the study. The large oak door was pulled tightly closed, but she could still clearly make out the voices of Ethan and Bennett.

"Please. This could ruin you, me, Amelia, everyone around you. It would be a disaster. He is an unethical man with more than just questionable associations."

"It won't be a disaster. Trust me. I know what I'm doing."

"I've already done that once, and look where it got me," Bennett retorted. "The entire city of Savannah has been wiped out with the financial collapse of the railroad holdings. Are you really so dense as to blame me for all of that? I'm flattered, really, but I can't actually take *all* the credit. I'm just one man."

Amelia could almost see Bennett's exasperation through the door.

"Don't be an idiot! Of course it is not all your fault, but you're not innocent either. You invested in a railroad to nowhere, and might I add, was never actually constructed, in competition with businesses with ten times your capital. Anyone with half an ounce of sense would have known that those were insurmountable odds, Ethan. You never had a chance. You lost everything you went with and more. In fact, from what I've seen in your records, almost double, which I can't understand. How many others did you pitch the railroad to that I didn't know about? Now they not only want their money back, they'll likely want your head on a stake for your failure as well. What you need to do is to beg for their mercy and pay them back when you can. Turning to a snake like Desoto is not a solution."

Amelia gasped out loud then covered her mouth, praying they hadn't heard her through the thick door. He couldn't mean Gabriel Desoto. There was no way Ethan would ever think of going into business with such a man. Desoto left nothing but carnage wherever he went and had more than once been a suspect of the suspicious disappearance of a man who had crossed him.

"I told you I will handle it."

"Yes, you *told* me that, but you haven't. And now they're coming after me for your debts. Who's next? Anyone else close to you with money? Michael Sullivan's got money. Is that why you're going through with the wedding to his daughter even though you know you should let her go? You're willing to ruin your fiancée's family too, as long as it gets you out of trouble."

Ethan scoffed. "Ruined! Why does everyone use that word? It's revolting! I haven't ruined a thing. Yes, we lost some momentum, but I can get it back just as quickly as I lost it, and then some! I just need your help. Like I said, it won't take much. Gabriel and I have all of the details worked out, if you just help me with the—"

"—And *I* said," Bennett interrupted, "I'm not authorizing another cent for the railroad. I'm through cleaning up your messes."

Hearing steps rapidly approaching the door, Amelia picked up her thick skirt and scooted around the corner as Bennett slid aside the door and stormed up the stairs. Ethan quickly followed, but Amelia stepped out and blocked his path. He tried to look unaffected by what had just happened, but she saw right through him.

"Ethan."

"Oh, did you find the scarf? I didn't see it in the dining room, so I set off to look elsewhere."

Not even waiting for her answer, he moved past her and put his hand on her elbow to guide her back towards the rest of her family in the library. She resisted.

"Ethan. I heard you and Bennett."

"Oh that? It was nothing, just a brotherly squabble."

"It wasn't nothing. I heard every word, although I'm having a hard time believing it. I thought you told me everything was not as bad as everyone said and that it was being blown out of proportion. Why did Bennett mention Gabriel Desoto? Ethan, he is a thief. You can't do business with him."

She grabbed his sleeves, her eyes begging him to listen to reason. If Bennett couldn't get through to him, surely she could. Ignoring her obvious pleas for forthrightness, he patted her hand as if she were a child and continued down the hall, "You misheard, Amelia. You were listening through a door. Eavesdropping, actually, but that's beside the point. Everything is fine. You have nothing to worry about."

She wouldn't let him skirt around the conversation this time. She stopped walking and stared at his back. "Don't insult me by telling me what I did or did not hear with my own ears, Ethan Bennigan. Please, be honest with me. That's all I've ever asked of you. I heard what Bennett said about you losing the money of men who are now rightfully angry. Think of what they could do to you. To your family! You have to tell someone. Tell my father. He will help you, I'm sure of it. Turning to someone like Gabriel Desoto will only deepen your troubles, not solve them."

His face flared red as he whirled on his heels and lunged to grab her shoulders. His grip was tight, and he towered over her so much that she had to crane her neck to look into his face. It was the same look she had seen in his eyes the day after his return, but she understood it more now. What initially came across as anger was actually desperation. Her instinct was to reach out for his hand, but then he gritted his teeth and spoke with such intensity and darkness she didn't dare open her mouth.

"Enough! Never tell me where or how or with whom I should acquire money again, Amelia. I will make the money, and you will spend it on your imported finery, or whatever you women spend our money on. That is how it will be. Where I get it is none of your business."

After he stalked back to the drawing room, Amelia stood absolutely still for more than a minute, her feet no more able to move than if they'd been crushed by the ferocity of the situation. She couldn't believe his nerve. To lie to her like that. And then to say it was none of her business when they were days away from their wedding was unbelievable. He asked her to trust him, but clearly he did not extend her the same courtesy.

Her paralysis soon deteriorated into an angry sob fighting to escape her throat. Embarrassed at her weakness, she ran back into the study and threw open the glass doors leading to the large rose garden and the pathway to the woods. She slowed to a walking pace right outside the house in case someone was to catch a glimpse of her through one of the large windows, but quickened her stride again within seconds to a sprint. She hadn't looked back until she had reached the river.

Even now, she was still furious about how he had spoken to her, but at least the initial adrenaline rush had eased, so she was able to walk the rest of the way back to her house at a reasonable speed after she retrieved her shoes from atop the log she'd left them when first entering the water. Still, she knew there would be serious questions when she got home since she hadn't told anyone where she was going when she had left in such a rush.

She crept through the well-pruned side garden planted in the traditional English style and quietly pushed open the large back service door leading into her family's home. Careful not to trip over the next day's meat that was soaking in pails of broth and water, she tiptoed up to the interior of the house. She tried to enter the bedroom hallway undetected via the servants' stairs but groaned when the old floor creaked under her feet. Thankfully, the door that flew open seconds later was not her parents' door, but Adele's.

"Amelia! Where have you been?" she hissed, yanking Amelia into the room and shutting the door.

"Ethan said you weren't feeling well and had gone home, but then you weren't here when we came back. I saw you leave his house alone, so I lied to Mother and told her you were already asleep when I checked on you in your room."

Amelia looked at her younger sister in her wrinkled cotton nightgown with her long blonde hair falling messily around her shoulders and realized that she must have been gone longer than she thought because Adele had been in bed for quite some time.

"I'm fine, Adele. I felt ill after dinner and just needed some air. I took a wrong turn and it took a while to find my way back to the path. I'm so sorry to have worried you." She smiled and turned to walk out the door.

"Amelia Faith Sullivan, you know those woods better than I do, and I would never get lost between Ethan's house and here, even in a blizzard. I do not believe you for a second."

Amelia smirked in spite of herself.

"You aren't leaving this room until you tell me where you really were because you are soaking wet. It didn't rain tonight."

Amelia had completely forgotten about her muddy dress. She looked at Adele whose huge brown eyes, one of her many stunning features, were searching hers for an answer. Amelia sighed.

"All right, I'll tell you, but you must promise not to mention any of this to Mother and Father."

Amelia sank down on the bed, letting her feet and knees hang over the edge as she flopped back onto the mattress, Adele following suit. She told Adele about

14

everything that had happened since Ethan arrived back in Moon Springs, including how much he had tried to hide his feelings and concerns and how he had angrily told her that it was none of her business as if she were just another society gossip.

Adele listened with her typical sincerity and then lay thoughtfully for a minute before propping up onto her elbow. "Maybe he's right."

Amelia bolted upright to look at her. "Of course he's not right! It is absolutely my business because in less than a month we will be married, and my name and money will forever be tied to his. And, if he is in danger from those men Bennett was talking about and thinking of turning to Gabriel Desoto to help him out of it, I have all the more reason to worry about him!"

Adele frowned. "It's not that I think you shouldn't be concerned. I just meant that maybe suggesting talking to Father was not the best thing to do. I'm sure there are things about Ethan's money and finances that you can't possibly understand, so without having the whole grasp of things, it may not be your place to give uneducated opinions."

Amelia crossed her arms in disgust, forgetting for the moment her unhappy situation and annoyed with her sister's obvious lack of desire for social progress. "Please do not tell me that Mother has convinced you that women have no place in a family's financial doings. How archaic."

Adele laughed. "Well, in this case, it makes sense. Women are not educated in business, and, therefore, just as we would scoff at a man giving his opinion on the latest fashions, we should not overreach when it comes to vocalizing our thoughts on things we know little about. Honestly, I think you should do as Ethan asks and trust him. I'm sure it really isn't as bad as it all seems. Bennett was probably exaggerating anyway. You know them, always trying to compete with each other to be biggest and the best at everything. From hunting to chess, days are never lacking in drama between those two. They were just caught in the heat of the moment, just as Ethan said. I wouldn't think any more about it tonight."

Amelia tried to remember her sister's advice as she climbed into her own bed moments later, but she couldn't shake her uncertainty. She silently prayed that Adele was right and that Bennett had overreacted, but deep inside she knew he hadn't.

Chapter 2

Three weeks later, Amelia had almost, but not quite, forgiven Ethan for the insanity of those first few days following his return. The morning after the confrontation at his house, he rushed to Sullivan's Pine at an almost indecent hour and apologized profusely for the tone he had taken with her. Although he did not promise to avoid business with Gabriel Desoto, he did vow to look into other options as well, which satisfied Amelia's greatest fear, but still left her harboring a slight distaste towards how he approached their impending marital partnership. Nevertheless, after the partial resolution, she found herself much more easily able to enjoy planning those tedious last minute details of their wedding which had become much more than the intimate occasion she had always dreamed of.

She had wanted to wed in a small ceremony among the tall Georgia pines beyond the house or perhaps at the front of the small chapel in the village with only family and a few close friends in attendance. It was her wedding day, so she didn't care about the social expectations of the wedding of a wealthy girl. She just wanted to be married with as little hassle as possible. But, unfortunately, that was not the way things were done in the household of Juliette Sullivan.

The European flair of her fully French-blooded mother didn't allow for anything to be done simply. She nearly collapsed in agony when Amelia had suggested the forest wedding and still was not appeased when the chapel was mentioned as an alternative.

"*Ma fifille,* no daughter of mine will wed in front of less than one hundred guests. Nellie O'Malley's daughter married with eleven attendants last summer, and we shall not be outdone by her."

"We, mother? I believe this is my wedding, and I'd like only Adele and May to attend me."

"You may be the one getting married, dear, but make no mistake—this is *my* wedding," Juliette smiled, and Amelia knew she believed it.

Juliette was nearly as complex as God can make a woman. She was, at the same time, the most gentle and yet fierce person Amelia knew. Obsessed with maintaining the traditions and morals brought over from the Old World, she fought for these with every ounce within her. So madly in love with her husband and her children, in her passionate desire to see the absolute best outcome for whatever situation her family found itself in, she seemed sometimes to come across to an outsider as being an upper-class snob.

Juliette's appearance, however, was uniformly beautiful. She was angelically pristine with a tiny frame, pale blond hair, grey eyes and nearly translucent skin. Amelia was certain her mother had not once sat in the sun for more than a second and usually felt like a chimney cleaner when near her, with her calloused skin and dirty fingernails from hours spent in the garden and the water. On the other hand, Adele closely resembled her mother, save the deep brown eyes she had inherited from their father, Michael. And even though she had spent many of the same years in the sun and woods with Amelia, Adele's skin still resembled that of a proper Southern Belle—smooth as silk and as ivory as the moon. Amelia hardly found that fair.

Juliette took great pains to select the perfect color of fabric for Adele to wear as the head attendant for the wedding. Complementary to Amelia's alabaster silk gown, she had chosen the palest of green taffeta fabric she could find when they visited Atlanta during the autumn. She instructed the seamstress to "enhance its beauty" through the hand-sewn addition of hundreds of pearls along the neckline and down the sleeves. It finally arrived two weeks before the wedding, and when Adele tried it on, Juliette felt justified in her instinct to go with the green.

"I really think it will reflect beautifully off the hazel in your eyes when you stand beside her, Amelia," Juliette smiled. "It's such a pity everyone wants a white gown for the bride these days, or we would have just used the green for you instead. Adele, you just be sure to never leave Amelia's side, and that should suffice."

"Millie," Adele said, "go and get your gown, and we'll try them on together. I'm sure they'll look stunning side by side!"

Amelia nodded and headed down the hall towards her room. She poked her head into the stairwell and called up to the third floor for one of the maids to come help her step into the dress.

The naturally tidy Nancy blanched at the sight of Amelia's messy room. Although it was cleaned by the staff almost daily, Amelia had the strangest ability to create havoc again by day's end with very little effort. Her dressing gown and slippers were tossed on the dark wood floor, and her towel from her morning bath was draped carelessly over the edge of her hand-carved mahogany bed while no less than a dozen books and catalogs were strewn in various spots around the room.

"Miss Amelia," Nancy cried, rushing immediately to remove the towel. "This will leave a mark, you know. And heaven help us all if your mother were to walk in upon this disaster!" scolded the young girl.

Smirking, Amelia reached for her wedding dress. The long train dragged heavily on the floor as she stood on her tiptoes to hang it upon the upper frame of her bed. She gently ran her fingers over the delicate bodice lace bundled silk bustle, and the expertly draped sleeves, picturing the moment when she would walk to the altar and marry Ethan, forever intertwining their lives.

Nancy ruined her whimsical moment by also bringing forth the bridal corset. Amelia groaned, "Nancy, can we please not use that today?"

Shaking her head, Nancy held the corset out towards her, "I'm sorry Miss Amelia, but I doubt your dress would even fit without it. Your mother sent such tight measurements to Paris, we'll need this just to squeeze you in it, I'm afraid. Don't worry, though, Miss, all the fashionable girls are wearing these, I'm told, so you'll fit right in. Sally Mae down at the Crawford farm says they're designed for these fancy occasions, to keep you nice and slim and sophisticated the way a proper young lady should be."

"You mean nice and slim and suffocated," Amelia retorted under her breath. She despised any sort of corset, but she had learned that arguing with her mother about such things was a lost cause and thus acquiesced to the horrid fashionable custom, though she still harbored hope that she would one day burn every single one she owned.

After being stuffed and tied into the extra-bone-lined cage and donning her ruffled petticoat, Nancy helped her step into the gown, careful not to pull or catch the fabric in any way. Once everything was assembled, Amelia had to admit that her mother was right. The dress was incredible. Flattering in every possible way, gracefully falling at just the right angles and setting off her complexion and figure in a way no other dress she'd ever donned had accomplished.

Suddenly overcome with a surprising shyness she didn't quite understand, she descended the stairs and quietly entered the sitting room where her mother and Adele waited. They turned as she approached them and each smiled with delight. Adele was rightfully thrilled with how her sister glowed, and Juliette also bore a slight smile of self-satisfaction that Amelia could attribute only to pride in having chosen such a tangible masterpiece.

"*Absolute magnifique!* Adele, stand next to your sister so I can see how they look together."

Adele obeyed and happily joined her sister. "Millie," she whispered, "You look absolutely perfect. Ethan won't know what to do with himself!"

Amelia blushed as her mother clasped her hands together and called for Nancy to wake May who was resting upstairs, anxious to show the girls off to anyone who would look.

Arriving a few moments later and looking much brighter with plumped cheeks for what Amelia assumed was the first time in her life, May was equally as excited to see the sisters in their gowns.

"Oh, Millie, it's stunning! I can't believe the wedding day is almost here! With everything that's been happening lately, I can't wait for a day to celebrate my brother instead of worrying about him." Tears pooled at the rims of her eyes.

"Oh, May, it will be all right. Ethan says it will be fine, and I'm trying to trust him, and you should too. He's smart, and I pray would never…"

"But Bennett said he won't let the railroad go. I'm so afraid that he'll lose even more money."

"May!" Juliette warned abruptly. "Let's not pretend we know anything about business. Women weren't meant for such things, so there's no point in worrying about it or trying to understand it. Everything will be fine. My husband will see to that, and that's all we need to know. Now, dears, shall we head to tea? Amelia, darling, please have Nancy help you change back into your day gown and join us in the sitting room." Juliette stood and briskly walked to the door, and all three girls knew there would be more scolding should they not follow closely behind. Holding her tongue until her mother was out of the room, Amelia still wanted to reassure May and so she squeezed her hand as they walked to the hall.

"It really will be okay, May. I didn't think so at first, either, but now I've made up my mind to trust Ethan like he asked me to."

May didn't look convinced, and Amelia still wasn't quite there herself, but she also knew that thinking about it anymore would send May back into hysterics, so she chose to push it out of her mind.

Later that evening all of the Sullivans gathered in the parlor to welcome the Bennigans to dinner. Michael Sullivan's sister, Louisa, and her husband, Patrick, also came over from their farm to join the dinner party. O'Brien's Plantation was a small, but well-managed, cotton and produce farm about two miles down the road from Sullivan's Pine that Patrick and Louisa maintained with the help of only a few farmhands and one cook.

Patrick acted not only as the property foreman but also as his own salesman and representative at the local markets and trading posts. It was clear to all who met him that not only did he take pride in his farming and the stable life it had provided to his family, but that it was his passion and, in almost every way, his life. As such, he had recently been elected the local representative for the Southern Farmers Alliance to the Populist Party.

The party had begun as a grassroots movement against the banking and railroad systems who forcibly lowered the agricultural prices at the expense of small farms. Members of the Populist Party purported that the greedy industry heads sought nothing less than the massacre of local farming livelihood in the name of modernity and ease of affordability. They could get crops shipped from South America and then cart them inland on a train more cheaply than they could buy them from farmers who needed to keep their prices high enough to make a minuscule profit to feed their families. Quality and tradition meant nothing.

It was here that his wife took objection to the whole concept. As the daughter of a merchant, Louisa had grown up wealthy and unattached to the **pride and passion** farming day in and day out over generations evoked. She loved her husband and the life they lived together on their quaint farm, but she cared little for how he made his money as long as he made it and certainly felt no emotional connection to the land itself. In fact, she tried to convince Patrick on several occasions that they should sell the farm and buy into Sullivan's Mercantile with her brother Michael, as he had offered numerous times in the past.

"We could keep the land and the house, and you could be home more often, not constantly exhausted, and of course much more cleanly dressed," she would tease. She had always been successful using her wit to convince practically everyone around her to cater to her desires, even when she was a child. Much to her frustration, Patrick seemed to be the only person alive who did not fall regularly under her spell.

The door opened as the housekeeper welcomed everyone into the entrance of the manor house. Louisa entered and happily greeted them each with a brief hug and a kiss, her skin flushed with anticipation of an elegant evening.

She embraced Amelia with an extra squeeze and whispered in her ear, "I am *so* glad you've had us to dinner. I'm nearly dying of boredom over all of this political talk Patrick goes on and on about, and I am anxious to hear the latest on your wedding plans."

Taking her cue from Juliette and Michael who quietly sat down at the head and foot of the table, everyone found their seats. Amelia sat down between Adele and May and across from Ethan who winked at her as she placed her napkin down upon her lap. Her face flushed in embarrassment. Adele was seated across from Bennett, so distracted he seemed to hardly notice he was dining somewhere other than his own home.

Juliette turned to May. "Where is Samuel? I would have thought he would be home from the mercantile hours ago."

Samuel and May lived in the caretaker's cottage at the back of the property and often came to the main house for dinner and conversation.

May laughed. "Oh, he was! He has just been working so hard building a crib for the baby, he said he couldn't possibly stop when he only had two more slats to insert. He asked us to go ahead without him."

Adele's eyes widened in amusement. "Samuel can't build!"

"I know. That's why it's taken him three months to make it! But I love him more for trying!"

Laughter filled the room just as the door from the kitchen swung open and Samuel, covered from head to toe in sawdust, rushed in, awkwardly tripping on the carpet as he flew to his seat.

"Sorry I'm late! Just got caught up on one of those blasted end panels! I don't know how carpenters get it right the first time."

Turning to his wife to plant a kiss on her cheek, he added, "May, I'm afraid our baby is going to be an only child."

"Oh?"

Samuel shrugged, "At the rate I'm making mistakes, it's going to take at least three more trees worth of wood to get this crib finished. I'm afraid we'd be Sullivan's Pine without the pine if I ever have to build anymore!"

The housekeeper entered with the first course of soup and ladled a large helping into everyone's bowl.

"Juliette, how are the wedding plans coming along?" Louisa asked.

Juliette proceeded to discuss every detail, down to the number of flowers she intended to use in Amelia's bouquet. The conversation had lasted throughout the entire dinner service and nearly into dessert when Michael Sullivan cleared his throat and announced, "I think that's enough wedding talk for now, my dear. I want to hear about Ethan's plans for the cottage in town I found for him and Amelia. How's it coming, my boy? I'd be happy to send over some of my workers in the evenings if you need some assistance finishing things up."

Ethan shook his head, "Thank you, sir, that is wonderfully kind of you, but I've already hired some locals to help me finish up before the wedding."

Watching her father mull over Ethan's response, Amelia could tell he was treading carefully when he responded, "Oh, well then, let me know if you need some assistance in any other way…"

"Oh, Papa," Amelia muttered and shook her head in frustration, seeing her fiancé's face lose all color.

Thankfully Ethan maintained his composure this time, a far better response than he had afforded her.

"You know, sir, with all due respect and gratitude, I do believe we're going to be fine in all regards. I've actually been discussing some very promising opportunities with some local investors—men with some fabulous connections here in Georgia and overseas."

Michael's face brightened, "Really? What industry strikes your fancy these days?"

Out of the corner of her eye, Amelia noticed Bennett shift uncomfortably in his seat as Ethan answered, "Actually, I'm still very passionate, sir, about the railroad industry. I think that if we shift our Provincial way of thinking, and perhaps form more of a coalition mentality, following in the worthy footsteps of our local farmers," he paused, nodding to Patrick, "I think we can bring locally accessible rail business to places even as small as Oak County."

Now it was Patrick's turn to perk up, "Imagine the business that could bring!"

Ethan nodded, and his voice quickened with enthusiasm. "Yes, that's exactly the thought. It could open up a whole new future for all of us, the need for more local crops, which would mean more business for you, Patrick, and of course more supply and demand for the Mercantile. The possibilities are truly limitless."

Amelia had to admire his passion, even if she didn't agree with his methods. That's one of the things she loved about him most. If he had his heart engaged, he gave the task his whole self, either to his benefit or detriment. Before she could worry it would be the latter, her thought process was interrupted by Bennett propelling his chair back from the table, the heavy wood scraping the floors, as he threw his napkin down on the table and stood to leave.

"I'm sorry, Mr. Sullivan," he said, turning and nodding to both of Amelia's parents, "Mrs. Sullivan, but I'm afraid I must bid you good evening. I won't sit here feigning civility another minute while my foolish brother spews childish ideas of grandeur and prosperity."

Michael, his face flushed a shade akin to that of his hair, stood suddenly as the room dropped into a stunned silence. "Bennett, sit down please. I will not tolerate such rudeness in my house."

Bennett shook his head and stood firm. "I'm afraid I will not, sir. It's not fair to you, to your family, and especially to Amelia to buy into his juvenile dreams that are misguided at best and more than likely dangerously under-thought. Ethan may not be troubled by associating our families and his future wife with criminal and unethical behaviors, but I most certainly am, and I will absolutely not tolerate it for another minute!"

Now Ethan stood to meet his brother square in the face and growled, "So that's it, is it? This is really all about Amelia! You claim I am not concerned about her future and, more ridiculously, that I toy with her safety? You must be out of your mind! I think of nothing but her day in and day out. I have nothing but her in my thoughts as I get up every day and make every decision that I do. It's all for her, and it's always been about her, and it *will* always be about her."

Her voice cracking, Amelia tried to reach across the table. "Ethan, please, sit down."

"No, Amelia." He curtly gestured for her to be quiet and glared at his brother. "Bennett seems to think it's his business how I provide for you, which is entirely false. He's not going to be your husband. I am."

Bennett unclenched his fists and stepped backwards.

"Ethan," he said in even and hushed tones, "You know that I wish nothing but absolute happiness for you and Amelia. I only want to see you both safe and sound and not under the influence of anyone unscrupulous."

She could see he meant to say something in retort, but Patrick and Michael took the reprieve in the argument to each take one of Ethan's arms.

"Come, Ethan!" Patrick said. "Let's move into the billiard room so you can tell me more about your railroad. Louisa's been telling me I need to sell the farm… Perhaps the railroad industry might treat me better!" He laughed in his usual jolly manner as the three men wandered off into the other part of the house. Samuel, who had remained his normal, peaceful self throughout the whole ordeal, also got up and kissed his wife on the cheek before following his father and uncle.

The remaining members of the now disastrous dinner party sat perfectly still, trying not to stare at Bennett who stood like a monument, unable to move towards the door or sit back in his chair. After what seemed like an eternity, Amelia whispered, "Bennett?"

He snapped out of his trance-like state and looked around the room almost seeming surprised to find half of the seats empty. He shook his head quickly and without saying another word strode decisively from the room. Amelia watched as he made his way towards the path at the back of the house that led to town through the woods.

Deciding that she'd suffered through enough unpleasant human interaction for one day, Amelia excused herself and went to her room for the night. She chose to dress herself for bed rather than call for one of the maids for something she was capable of doing alone. She did, however, remember Nancy's admonishment about her untidy room, and carefully folded her evening gown over the back of her dressing table chair before wearily creeping into her bed and closing her eyes.

She awoke after what felt like mere minutes with adrenaline pumping quickly through her veins, but as she looked at the moon high in the sky outside her window, it had been close to two hours since she'd lain down. She could have sworn she'd heard a shrill scream in her sleep. She was about to lie back down, certain that she had just been dreaming, when she heard it again, this time piercing the night with an unmistakable horror. It took her only seconds to realize that it was coming from the garden outside. She threw her shawl over her shoulders and rushed out of her room, not even bothering to put on her slippers.

She arrived at the back door of the house and saw her father about fifty paces ahead of her, still in his dinner clothes, rushing towards the small offshoot of the river that ran through the back of the garden. Following closely behind him, she ignored the damp coldness of the evening on her bare feet as she ran past the flowers and trees and was almost upon her father when someone stepped out in her way and grabbed her shoulders, stopping her from moving the final steps to where her father was on his knees, bending over to peer at something down at the water's edge.

"Amelia," her brother insisted, holding her arms firmly. "You can't go there."

Amelia turned to face her brother, still half asleep and utterly confused as to what was lying in the water that had sparked such fear in whoever had screamed. She could only assume there was a dead animal down the embankment, or even, upon a second glance at her brother's pale and glassy eyes, possibly a drifter who had slipped on the hill and drowned in the river. *It wouldn't be the first time*, she thought, as she tried to wiggle free from Samuel's strong arms.

"Sam, let me go! I want to see what's over there."

His voice grew uncharacteristically stern. "*No, Amelia.*"

She had never in her entire life heard her brother raise his voice to her like that. Her insides began to palpitate with growing concern as she looked around in the darkness to see that May was nowhere to be found.

Breathlessly she craned her neck down the path towards Samuel's cabin. "Oh, Samuel... Is it May?"

"May's fine, Amelia. I took her home earlier this evening because she was tired."

Absolutely relieved, she murmured, "Oh thank God," and again began walking towards the river.

This time, he grabbed her arm in his hand with a grip that was undeniably meant to stop her from moving another inch. She whirled around, ready to smack it away, when he whispered, "It's Ethan."

"What's Ethan?"

"Amelia," Samuel pulled her towards him, trying to wrap his little sister in his embrace, as if he could protect her from what he was about to say. "Ethan is...he's..." His voice was barely above a whisper. "In the water."

She heard him talking right beside her ear, but he suddenly sounded as if he was miles away, his voice a distant echo. The only thing she could hear and feel clearly was the rapidly increasing thudding of her heartbeat. That she heard without any trouble. It was like a pulsating hammer, drowning out all other sensations.

"What do you mean?" she managed.

The pity in his eyes spoke more than his words ever could as the realization of what he'd said hit her—body, mind, and soul—like a freight car. She turned towards the riverbank and looked, willing her legs to move to the edge to prove to her brother it couldn't possibly be Ethan that was causing all of the ruckus, but all she could manage to do was fall to her knees from where she stood in the middle of the pathway and stare in the direction of her father who had just noticed that she was there.

Michael's face twisted in sadness when he saw his daughter was there, and he scrambled to his feet at once and rushed to her side, trying to help her stand. Her legs didn't cooperate though, and they buckled again, sending her crashing back to the dirt, so he bent down to her level and gently eased her onto his knee, wrapping his arms around her as if she was an injured child. Overcome by his tenderness, she went almost limp in his arms as she pleaded softly, "Papa, please, help him."

Tears starting to run down his ruddy cheeks, Michael did his best to smooth out his daughter's hair as he whispered, "I'm so sorry, Millie."

Chapter 3

       The hours that followed were a blur of faces and voices constantly moving in and out of the house. Amelia saw it all from the loveseat in her mother's parlor, and yet not one instant of the chaos registered in her mind. Her father carried her in from the garden after Ethan's body had been discovered and set her on the soft chair, quickly covering her with a blanket since she had run out into the yard in her nightgown. Then he'd gone to fetch the doctor to attend to Ethan's body. Her mother, also awakened by the screams, sent the stablehand to Louisa's house, bringing her back in hopes that she could help care for her understandably shocked niece. Louisa burst into the house an hour later and rushed to the loveseat, cupping both of her hands to Amelia's cheeks and kissing her forehead.

       "Oh my heart. I can hardly believe it!"

       Amelia thanked her numbly, for what, she wasn't entirely sure, and then subsequently seemed to have lost all ability to communicate, as if the arrival of her aunt in the middle of the night made things that had been entirely imagined suddenly feel very real.

       Nearly six hours later, Amelia still hadn't left that spot on the couch. The maid tried several times to give her tea and bread, but she hadn't even registered her presence. When her mother insisted she put on some warmer clothes, she rigidly allowed Aunt Louisa and Adele to change her into a day dress, but they'd had to shimmy her nightgown out from underneath her as she sat. All this time, she'd never uttered a word as she stared at the massive oak door to the room that led to the front hallway of the house.

Louisa observed Amelia's glassy eyes dart to the front door every time it opened and follow whoever it was until she could no longer see the person in the hallway; then her eyes would move back to their post at the door, as if eagerly anticipating a new arrival.

"Amelia, you need to get some rest. Let me take you to your room."

Amelia shook her head violently and immediately locked her eyes back on the door.

Louisa looked to Adele for help, who gently touched her sister's shoulder, trying to coax her back to reality.

"Millie... It won't be Ethan."

Amelia broke her fixation briefly, her face showing tired confusion as if she had just now realized she was not alone in the room. Still, she did not meet Adele's eyes and did not move.

"The next person to come in," Adele continued slowly, easing herself onto the seat next to her. "No matter who it is...won't be Ethan."

Amelia sat there for several more minutes, her mouth frowning slightly while considering whether or not to submit to her sister's words. She squinted at her aunt and sister, who both looked back at her, then back at the door again. This sequence repeated itself several more times until, to everyone's surprise, she glanced once more at the door and suddenly stood. Adele quickly joined her and wrapped her arms around her sister's shoulders as Amelia, without uttering a sound, exited out into the hallway and stepped onto the first of main stairs.

As she slowly ascended the broad wooden staircase, she paused to look down into the hall and caught the eyes of her mother, who was whispering in hushed tones with her father and the doctor. Juliette, generally an expert at hiding any sort of emotion outside the privacy of her innermost circle and, on a bad day, the occasional maid, had tears brimming in her eyes as she met the gaze of her daughter.

Seeing her mother's uncharacteristic public display of emotion seemed to shock Amelia out of her hypnosis, and she felt her cheeks burning with hot tears. She frantically looked upward to count the steps ahead of her and resolved that she must get to her bedroom before any stranger, and now there were several in the house, saw her cry. But she only managed to take two more steps before her legs betrayed her. Reaching instinctively for the rail, she collapsed with an unladylike thud that paled in comparison to the loud sob she heard escape her mouth. Both out of concern for her sister's safety and also desperately trying to help her avoid an embarrassing spectacle, Adele quickly gathered her up in her arms as Juliette gasped and rushed up the stairs to grab her daughter's other arm. The two women coaxed her up the last few steps and gingerly down the hallway into her room.

Once there, Amelia barely made it to her bed before folding over again in tears. Her fingers gripping the sheets so tightly her knuckles turned white, she cried unabashedly for nearly five minutes as she finally allowed herself to process the events of the past hours.

At one point, she tried to sit up, but only managed to shift her head slightly to meet her mother's sorrowful eyes. "Why?"

She had only managed a single word, but it may well have been a thousand because the answer was no less difficult. Gently moving her daughter's tear-soaked hair away from her eyes, Juliette leaned forward and covered Amelia's body with hers.

"Only God himself knows, *ma fifille.*"

Amelia turned her face back to the wall and continued weeping. Looking helplessly at her mother, Adele waited for some suggestion as to what to do to help her poor sister, but Juliette only shook her head sadly and continued to gently rub Amelia's back until she fell into a fitful, exhausted sleep.

When she awoke in a smothering darkness blanketed in silence several hours later, she thought everything had just been a horrible nightmare, but then she felt her sister's warm body shift beside her on the bed, and she realized it had all been painfully real. Willing herself to sit up, she tried to ease out of the big canopy bed, but as she stood slowly, Adele reached out and grabbed her hand.

"Millie, please lie down. Mother is worried you'll take ill if you don't get more rest."

Tugging her hand out of Adele's grasp, Amelia grabbed her shawl and quickly wrapped it around her body, shivering from the kind of chill that stemmed from death and sadness she knew innately would not cease even with the soft knit of the garment hugging her body.

"I'm hungry, Adele," she lied.

She couldn't eat a bite of food, but she needed to get out of that house. She needed to be able to think clearly, to process what had transpired. She couldn't do that here. She needed fresh air.

"Then let me come with you, to help you down the stairs," Adele interrupted her thoughts, swiftly standing and grabbing her own shawl.

Assisting her sister carefully down the back stairs to the kitchen, Adele tried to convince Amelia to sit at the table and eat some warm beef broth that the cook had prepared for the extra people who had been swarming the house since the discovery of Ethan's body. Admittedly, it smelled delicious, but Amelia declined.

"I can tell you're cold, and you haven't eaten in hours. Please eat some," Adele insisted firmly.

Amelia shook her head, gesturing instead to the shelf of leftover food from yesterday. "Let's put some food in a basket and take it to the river."

"The river? Oh Millie, you can't. It's nighttime." Adele pointed to the dusk settling outside the small stone window. The kitchen was halfway below ground, but had a window at grass level, and Amelia could see her sister was right. She had slept the entire day.

Realizing how hungry she was after moving around, and deciding the coming darkness did not concern her, Amelia grabbed a basket from a shelf and began loading it with what she thought she might be able to stomach—a small loaf of French bread and some hard, white cheese. She also filled a jar with water from the barrel and headed towards the door. She turned to look at her sister who gazed upon her with such sincere concern she couldn't decide if Adele feared she was insane or just stupid.

"You can come with me. I wouldn't mind the company. I just need to be outside for a bit. I promise we won't be gone long."

Shrugging her shoulders in defeat, Adele acquiesced and climbed the small stone steps up to her sister in the garden. Knowing their mother would lose her senses if she saw them out without a chaperone so late in the evening, the girls quickly hurried away from the warm light glowing from the immense house and into the woods.

For a beautiful moment, it was as if they were little girls again, dashing to escape from their pesky brother and cousins who were chasing them with sticks, pretending they were dragons. She had assumed, naively it now seemed, that she and Ethan would be chasing their own children through these woods towards the river one day. Now that would never happen. That dream had died with Ethan. She wondered how many other dreams she would have to bury in the coming days.

They arrived at their favorite overlook of the river within minutes and settled down on the grass. Adele moved aside the soft fabric lining the basket and took out the bread. She broke off a small piece of the loaf and handed it to Amelia, who chewed it unenthusiastically, ignoring the pleasant taste. She stared into the peaceful deepness of the briskly flowing water and leaned her head wearily upon Adele's shoulder.

They sat in silence for several minutes before she said, "It seems so unfair, don't you think, that Ethan should have to die in such a place. Why this river? Why would the very place I cherish the most take the man I love?"

Her tears returned, and she dabbed at them with a napkin. She hated feeling this way. She wasn't fragile. She was the strong one. She was the one to bravely wipe the tears away from her sister's or May's face when something bad happened. When she had fallen as a child, she'd never cried. Physical pain didn't bother her, but this—this raw ache that consumed her—she didn't know how to handle it. "The river didn't do this to Ethan, Millie."

Nodding, Amelia glanced at her sister, emerging out of the troubled depths of her mind.

"I know. But I just can't understand it. Ethan knows how to swim. And he was so sure-footed. I can't possibly imagine how he could have slipped in that spot. He must have traveled down that path hundreds of times, even in the dark."

"No, Amelia, that's not what I mean," Adele said, turning her face towards the reflection of the moon now high in the evening sky, its silver beams shining brightly on the water. She sat for a moment, unconsciously twirling the tie of her dress around her fingers, deep in thought, as if considering whether or not to continue.

"Then speak plainly." Amelia sensed Adele struggled terribly over whether or not to say anymore, but she couldn't imagine why.

"He didn't drown, Millie. He was hit over the head. He was…" She paused again, and looked directly into her sister's face, unwilling to speak the word that Amelia herself now had to utter.

"Murdered?"

She had never even considered that it was anything except a horrendous accident.

"How do you know that?"

"The doctor told Father and Mother after they pulled Ethan up out of the river. There was a gash," she gestured to the back of her head, "the doctor said it was not caused by anything around the body. He had cuts and bruises on his face befitting of the rocks where he was lying. But the wound on the back of his head was caused by something else."

"They're sure? He couldn't have hit his head somewhere else?"

"Yes. Sheriff Hastings arrived soon after the doctor shared his suspicions. He found a large rock a bit further down the path. It was covered in blood. They think whoever did it intended to take it and throw it further down where the creek meets the river but dropped it when the maid screamed, and they had to run."

"Maid?"

Amelia hadn't even thought to ask who had been the source of the shriek that had woken her from her sleep the night before.

"Nancy. She was coming back from visiting her sister in town, and she discovered Ethan's body in the creek."

41

Poor Nancy, Amelia thought. But, more pressingly, who would have wanted Ethan dead? Even as she asked herself that question, she had to admit there were dozens of people who were certainly angry with him over his financial misfortune. She didn't know the exact names of the families who had been affected by his losses in Savannah or the extent to which their estates had dwindled at the hands of Ethan, but she was certain that any number of them could have been angry enough to cause him harm over it. People had killed for far less.

"I need to look at his records," Amelia announced.

Adele eyed her quizzically. "His what?"

"His business records. To see whose money he lost in Savannah. It has to be one of them. No one else would have wanted to hurt him and also had the knowledge and access to where he was last night."

"You don't know that, Amelia. Maybe it was one of his business partners from the railroad. I'm sure they're not decorated citizens."

Amelia frowned. "But they would have had to follow him closely for the entire day without being seen, and then wait for him to leave our house alone, hit him with a rock, and then escape abruptly undetected in the utter darkness. That seems like an awfully daunting task for someone not from here, don't you think?"

Now Adele frowned. "I'm not sure, but what I do know is that this is the worst thing for you to be thinking of right now, Millie. The only thing you need to worry about now is rest. Come now, we need to get home and get you to bed."

"I need to do *something* to help, Adele. I'll go mad otherwise. I have to figure out what happened to him."

"No. Leave that to Sheriff Hastings. What you need to do is allow yourself time to process what has happened, and then, as much as you hate to do it, you need to allow yourself to grieve, Millie."

Amelia gazed back out to the river, unwilling to let Adele's words take root in her mind where she knew they would reap and sow only sadness. She couldn't think about grief now. Grief was unproductive. But she didn't have the strength to argue with her sister, so she acquiesced to her request and they gathered up their belongings and began the walk back towards their house.

When they came to the footpath that led to the garden near where Ethan had been found, Amelia hesitated.

"Why don't we take the roadway, Millie?" Adele suggested.

Shaking her head, Amelia started down the path.

"It's not that. I'm fine to walk this way. It's just, as I see this path, I realize that there are so few people who would actually think to use this to come to and from town. There is the family, of course. And some of the servants. But other than that, no one else would even think to use it as a thoroughfare to the house. And Ethan arrived at our house with Bennett via the road."

Following her sister's train of thought, Adele added, "So whoever hurt Ethan would have either had to follow him closely while we were at dinner or be extremely familiar with our property themselves."

"Right, because otherwise, they would have expected him to leave by the road as he had come. So, if it was a stranger, he must have been outside or inside the house the whole time."

Amelia shuddered thinking of a murderer hiding away in their home while her family innocently dined the evening away. But then she stopped and looked ahead into the darkness.

As if reading her mind, Adele looked in the same direction, "Millie, you *are* thinking it was a stranger? It would have to be. You don't think it could actually be someone Ethan knew well? No one we know would want to hurt Ethan."

"Of course. It had to have been someone either angry with him over what happened in Savannah or someone he didn't know at all. Or perhaps he came upon a robber or someone else who shouldn't have been on the path..." Her voice trailing, Amelia halted abruptly, causing Adele to nearly collide with her from behind.

Grabbing her sister's arm, Adele whispered, "What is it Millie? Did you see something?"

Amelia didn't answer. Not because she didn't want to, but because she couldn't put what she was feeling at that moment into words. She stared down the path towards the house where a tiny beam of light shone from the blackness.

It had been like a flash of lightning. A glimmer of a memory, there and gone in an instant. A vision, almost. Her heart screamed at her that it meant nothing, but she also couldn't pinpoint why she had remembered it at that exact moment.

Perplexed, Adele whispered again, "What is it Amelia?"

Turning back to her sister, Amelia tried to assuage her. "It's nothing."

"It can't be nothing. You look like you've seen a ghost!"

Feeling as if she actually had, Amelia stepped to the side of the path, pulled her skirt to the side and kneeled down to sit on a fallen log.

"It's just that Ethan wasn't the only one on that path last night."

"Of course not. Nancy found him, so she was there too. And whoever killed him was also. But like you said, it had to have been someone who followed him there after he left."

"No, I mean I *know* someone else was on that path. I saw them go. They could have waited for Ethan," Amelia said quietly, closing her eyes as if wishing the memory away, because it was too horrible to even consider.

"Who? Who did you see, Millie?" Adele urged.
"Bennett."

Chapter 4

     Snuggled again closely to her sister, Amelia was able to get a small amount of rest that night. Although she still took excellent care of her, Adele had been extremely quiet as they had finished their journey back to the house and prepared for bed. Her uncharacteristically creased brow revealed a soulful weariness that had catapulted her well beyond her years. Amelia hated that she had caused her sister such turmoil and was still reeling from the wound she'd received by her own unwilling initiation into a world of terror and sadness. But she also knew she couldn't ignore the fact that she had seen Bennett go down that path when he had left the dinner just because it could hurt her sister. She tried to explain as much when Adele blew out the candle and silently slid under the warm sheet and down blanket.

     "Adele, I love him, too, you know." Feeling her sister's body tense up suddenly, Amelia felt the need to explain further. "Bennett...I mean. I love him. But not in the way that you do."

     Adele rolled over to face her. "Amelia, I don't..."

     Amelia put her hand over her sister's mouth.

     "Yes, you do. There's no need to try and hide it, from us or yourself. We can all see it plainly."

     Adele's eyes glistened. "It wasn't him who killed Ethan. I know it's wasn't! He would *never* hurt anyone. Please, you know him. You know he wouldn't do this," she pleaded.

"I certainly hope he wouldn't, but we don't know he didn't. And I saw him go down that path when he left. Besides, he was undeniably upset with Ethan. I'm sorry. I cannot hide that from Father and Sheriff Hastings if they ask me whom I saw. I will have to tell them."

"Amelia, no!" Adele cried.

"He's my dearest friend, Adele; I wouldn't do this if I didn't think it was necessary. But he was so angry. And he knows that Ethan would have gone that way if he was alone. I hate that we're even discussing this, but it fits the exact scenario we talked about."

"But he could go to jail!"

"Better jail than the grave, Adele." Amelia snapped, instantly regretting her thoughtless words.

She heard her sister gasp. Amelia sat up in bed and struck another match to relight her candle. She reached over to Adele, who clung to her pillow, her body turned away from her in rebellion.

"I am so sorry. That was a horrible thing to say. I don't know what's wrong with me."

Brushing her tears from her cheeks, Adele nodded. "It's okay. It's been such a long day. I'm sorry I was being so selfish. Of course you want to know who did it. I shouldn't have asked you to hide what you saw. I'm just scared for Bennett. I know he didn't do it, and I don't want him to have to go through more than he already is. You lost your fiancé, but he lost his brother."

Amelia hadn't thought about it that way. In that sense, she too had been thinking selfishly, wanting justice for Ethan without considering how the others around her were feeling. And if she was being honest, she didn't actually think Bennett was capable of killing Ethan. Still, she knew she had to tell her father.

The next morning dawned gray and chilly. Nancy had been given some time off after her wretched discovery, so the downstairs maid, Fanny, helped both girls dress in their darkly colored mourning clothes she'd pulled from the attic, and the sisters descended the stairs to the dining room. Amelia had planned to talk with her father first thing, but she stopped when she found Samuel and May already at the table.

May, eyes puffy and swollen, stood and rushed to her.

"Amelia!"

Mindful of her conversation with her sister the previous night, Amelia hugged the frail girl tightly, less for her own sake and more out of support for the fragile being now clinging to her sleeves.

"I'm so sorry, May," she whispered through tears.

"He loved you," May managed.

"Thank you," she pulled back away from her sister-in-law to gently touch her face, wiping away her tears.

Trying, weakly, to lighten the mood for May's sake, Amelia looked towards the table. "Are you able to eat anything?"

May nodded. "The baby doesn't seem to realize I'm grieving," she almost laughed. "I'm starving."

Amelia forced a smile and sat down at the table, taking a small bit of food for her own plate. Adele sat down across from her, nervously picking at her food and continuously looking back and forth from her sister to her father. Amelia noted her concern and gave a small smile of reassurance. She wouldn't bring up Bennett now. Not in front of her sister or May. That would be too much for both of them.

Juliette, much more composed than she had been the day before, dabbed at her face with her napkin.

"Amelia, dear, May has kindly offered to allow you to plan Ethan's funeral."

"Oh May, are you sure?" Amelia questioned.

"Of course! It's what he would have wanted. And to be honest, I'm not sure I could do it. I'm just so sad and tired, and Bennett, well, he won't even let me breathe Ethan's name right now, so I know he couldn't do it."

Amelia unconsciously looked up at Adele to see her reaction and saw that her sister's face had paled considerably. She forced herself to hide the misgivings creeping into her mind and nodded to May.

"Absolutely. I'd be proud to do it."

After breakfast concluded, Amelia touched her father softly on the shoulder. "Papa, I'd like a word with you, please, privately."

"Of course, my girl," Michael said, pushing away from the table and heading towards the study opposite the dining room.

Following closely behind, Amelia could feel Adele's eyes burning into her from behind. She hated what she had to do but knew there was no other choice. Her father grabbed his pipe and found his seat quickly in his favorite over-stuffed chair beside the great stone fireplace. He seemed completely at home here in this room. As much as Juliette had the decorative dominion over the rest of their expansive antebellum home, she had relinquished all control of the study to her husband, and he had flourished with the freedom. The cozy room was covered wall-to-wall and floor-to-ceiling on three sides with dark mahogany bookshelves. The wall that didn't have shelves was dark, too, because her father had chosen to cover the windows with velvet curtains dyed to a deep, ruby red. In addition to the antique books and globe on a gold stand near his desk, Michael had also mounted several deer and elk heads around the room, and a massive bear skin rug warmed the center of the old wooden floor.

Because of its lack of natural light, a fire provided a gentle glow for the room nearly year-round, so the children could always count on it being the same —the same smells, the same feelings, the same warmth. It was by far Amelia's favorite room in the house. Over the years it had given her a sense of security and safety she felt nowhere else. Today, though, as she took a seat on the chair closest to the fire, that sense of safety was gone, and she feared she might never feel that way again, even in the comfort of her own home.

Michael cleared his throat. "How are you doing this morning?"

"I am managing, I suppose," Amelia began nervously, "but there is something of some difficulty I need to bring to your attention."

She couldn't make herself look at him directly. She felt almost as if she was about to announce she suspected his own son of the murder. Michael loved Bennett, May, and Ethan as if they were his own, especially since the death of their parents eight years before during an outbreak of scarlet fever.

"Oh?" his eyebrows arched with curiosity.

Amelia decided she needed to just say it, so she blurted, "I saw Bennett go onto the path that night when he left the house. He didn't go back down the road, Father—he went down the path. And he was…so, so *angry* when he left. So, I fear…" she trailed off, hoping she wouldn't actually need to utter the words.

"You think Bennett may have killed Ethan?" her father mercifully finished for her.

Now she was able to look him in the eye. "I hope not, father, I really do. But he was so upset with Ethan."

Michael frowned, "I do agree he seemed at odds with Ethan, but I seriously doubt he was angry enough over one tense dinner to kill his brother."

Relieved that he thought so, Amelia got to her feet and was about to take her leave when she suddenly remembered the argument she'd overheard at Ethan's a few days before the murder. She sank back down into the chair.

"You disagree, Amelia?"

She briefly recalled the events of the discussion the brothers had had. Michael raised his hand suddenly when she mentioned Gabriel Desoto's name. "Now hold on, Amelia. Ethan promised me just two days before our dinner that he hadn't yet invested with

Desoto. He gave me his word, in fact, that he would not because I didn't think it was wise. Bennett must have been mistaken."

"But, you see, that's just it. When they were fighting that night, Bennett claimed Ethan had already entered a contract with Desoto."

"Did you ask him about it?"

"Yes…" she answered slowly. "And he'd denied it. He said I'd misheard him."

"There you have it! It must have been a mistake on Bennett's part, and so there's no reason to think he would hurt Ethan. Come now, my dear," he stood and walked to the door, "you need not trouble yourself further with such dark thoughts. We have a wonderful sheriff here, and he will do his best to find Ethan's killer." He paused in the doorway, "I do think, however, that we must accept that we may never know who actually did it. It could have been a drifter seizing on a potential robbery victim. Poor lad. I doubt Ethan even had a penny on his person. Such a senseless thing," he sighed, shaking his head as he left the room.

Amelia stayed for a few moments, trying to decide what to do next. She could take her father at his word and wisdom and trust that he was right and that Bennett had simply misunderstood Ethan's plans. Doing so would allow her time to properly grieve for Ethan without distraction. That would undoubtedly be the safest thing to do. But, if she was honest with herself, she knew that she could never sit back and let things play out their course. She knew she hadn't misheard Bennett and Ethan the night they had argued. And she had without a doubt seen Bennett leave her house and head down the path the night Ethan died. She stood up, smoothing out her skirt. She had decided. She must find out for herself.

Under the guise that she would be looking through his desk for passages and scripture for Ethan's funeral among his notes, Amelia secured a key to the Bennigan Financial Advisory office in town from May the next day. As the carriage slowed in front of the door, she had to motivate herself to step down and move toward the door. A hard, chilly rain had begun to fall during her journey to town, creating small puddles she carefully avoided as she made her way up the cobblestone path to the door. A rustic clay tile roof overhung the front stoop, and water poured liberally over the edge as she ducked quickly inside.

The dark room was eerily silent and cold. She surveyed the small office, trying to decide what to do first. Similar to her father's study, Amelia had always maintained a fond affection for this small but tidy building where Ethan and Bennett conducted their business. They had taken over for their father when he'd passed away and had stretched their reach far beyond Oak County over the years. There were two desks on opposite sides in the front room where each man sat. There were bookshelves behind each desk and a filing system for their respective client papers. In the back corner near the stairs that led up to the storage attic was a small wood-burning stove that they used to heat the space which was flanked by a few simple, yet comfortable, chairs for their clients and guests. Amelia was chilled to the bone, so she lit a small fire and sat down on the chair facing out into the room until she warmed up. She did intend to find scripture for the funeral while there, so she decided to look for those first, and then see what else she might come upon in the process.

She slowly crossed the room to the bookshelf next to Ethan's desk. Running her fingers along the spines of each book, she inhaled the scent of the ancient jackets and fondly recalled how much Ethan had loved to read. She took one from the shelf and fingered through the pages. Notes were written furiously in every margin. She replaced the book and picked another from the shelf. She found the same attention to detail in Ethan's personal notes in each subsequent book she pulled from the shelf and feverishly read each and every one, relishing in the thoughts of this man that she so cherished. As she read, she could almost hear his strong voice speaking the words. For a moment, it was as if he was here with her, divulging his deepest musings. Wiping away the tears she hadn't even realized had fallen onto the collection of Old English poetry translations she was holding, she turned to look for a cloth to dab her face when the door to the building suddenly flew open and a tall figure jumped inside and slammed the door behind him in a poor effort to keep out the now howling wind and rain.

Amelia let out a startled cry, and she ran behind the desk, making sure there was ample space between herself and the stranger.

The man instinctively held up his hands in surrender. "I'm sorry! I've startled you. I didn't realize someone would be in here."

"Who are you?" Amelia demanded.

"Devon Bennigan, ma'am," he said and held out his hand.

"Devon?" Recognition slowly spread across her face as she remembered Ethan's older cousin who had spent several summers living with him. But the man who stood before her looked nothing like the tall, gangly boy she recalled.

She held out her hand and shook his warmly. "Amelia."

Sadness softened his expression as he nodded. "You have my sincerest condolences, Amelia."

"Thank you." Her eyes met his for a brief moment before darting away again with a blush.

He reminded her too much of Ethan. They had nearly the same face and the same eyes, except Devon's were darker than Ethan's emerald ones had been. Devon's eyes reminded her of warm chestnuts. Still, it was almost as if she was seeing Ethan himself. The similarity unnerved her, and she shuddered.

"Um, are you cold?"Devon took off his overcoat and hung it near the door, then removed his suit jacket and offered it to her.

She was chilly but shook her head and smiled. "Thank you, but no. I am simply shocked at how much you've grown!"

He laughed softly. "You have as well. I think that's to be expected."

It was her turn to laugh. He had always been the comical one of his family, maintaining his light-hearted enjoyment of life throughout even the darkest of circumstances. His mother had died when he was very young, and his father, an officer of the United

States Navy, was seldom home, so he spent the school year away at boarding schools in Savannah and summers at Morrow House with his cousins until the year their parents, too, had died. Amelia had always, even from a young age, imagined that must have been an extremely lonely way to grow up, and she had always pitied him for that, yet she admired the way he had handled it with such gracious humor.

Catching herself laughing at such a time suddenly made her feel very guilty, so Amelia looked away, gesturing to the desk. "I believe May mentioned to me that you may be coming in to help Bennett organize Ethan's business papers. I know they are grateful for the help."

"I'm happy to do what I can," he said soberly, "but I must admit, I'm not sure how much help I'll be. I know very little about their business."

"Perhaps I can help you get started?" Amelia asked.

Gratefully, Devon pulled a second chair to the desk, and they sat down to begin the daunting task. The conversation started lightly as the old friends caught up on the past several years. She learned that he had studied law at the College of Charleston and had been practicing in Savannah for five years.

"It has worked out well for me. I essentially work for myself, so I'm able to be away for extended periods of time to travel or when other matters need my attention."

"Well, I know that May is so happy you were able to come on such short notice. Bennett has been," she paused to choose her words carefully, "unable to focus on business affairs since Ethan... passed," she finally managed.

"I can imagine," Devon responded absently. He was intently studying a particular notebook that he'd pulled from under a stack of papers. Amelia leaned over and saw that it was a bank ledger with Ethan's handwriting scribbled haphazardly on the page.

"Do you see anything of importance?" she inquired.

He cleared his throat. "Well, as I said, I'm not at all familiar with their business, but it would appear that Ethan was indeed substantially in debt, even with the help of your father."

"My father? No, that can't be right. Ethan refused his assistance on numerous occasions. I heard him myself."

"Well, it says here that he was borrowing several hundred dollars a month from your father for the past year."

She snatched the book from his hands to see for herself.

"I don't understand. They both implied every time it was discussed that it was simply a proposition, not a bona fide agreement. It doesn't make sense."

She slumped, frustrated, into her chair and stared at the book.

"Perhaps he was just offering him more help?"

"Possibly. Still, I can't believe they both deceived me, especially since it was my idea in the first place."

"Pardon my presumptiveness, Amelia, but I'm sure they just didn't want to worry you about financial matters. Generally, it's not considered a woman's concern."

Forgetting her manners, she straightened up, exasperated. "Oh, not you too!"

"I said generally. I happen to think it's every bit as much of a wife's concern as her husband's when it comes to the financial standings of a family business. And you were nearly Ethan's wife. So, yes, I can see that would be extremely frustrating for you," he allowed, amused at her feistiness.

Amelia relaxed and sat back, satisfied. Still, she knew this revelation got them no closer to finding who killed Ethan. Her father certainly had nothing to do with it. He wouldn't want Ethan dead if he'd been investing with him. There would be no purpose in that. Besides, he was her father.

Devon's voice broke through her thoughts. "Amelia, come over here."

She hadn't even noticed him get up from the desk, but now he was across the room at the bookshelf where she had been before he'd arrived. He had pushed aside a few books to reveal a large envelope tucked behind them.

"I thought maybe I'd find some older records over here, but I've found this. It's unmarked and sealed."

"How strange," she remarked. "We may as well open it. Ethan has no need for secrets anymore."

Devon walked back to the desk and sat down to retrieve the letter opener. He carefully opened the seal and pulled out a small black book. "It's another ledger."

Opening the cover, they saw the year 1892 written on the first page.

"It's from this year," Amelia frowned."That doesn't make any sense. Why would he have two separate ledgers for the same year?"

"I can't be sure, but this book seems to be dedicated to business outside of this county," he explained, pointing to several Savannah addresses in the address section at the back of the book.

"These must be related to his dealings with the railroads," she said.

"Apparently," he frowned.

She sat quietly and allowed Devon to examine the book more thoroughly. After several minutes he looked up and sighed. "It seems his financial debt was more than anyone realized. The amounts notated here exceed the totals May and Bennett related to me by tens of thousands of dollars."

Amelia gasped,"You mean the amount he lost?"

"Yes."

He showed her transactions dating back over the six months that amounted to several local businessmen investing thousands a piece. This changed everything. If he had lost even more than he'd originally let on, some of these men could have lost their entire life's savings. That could be enough to drive any one of them to kill him.

"And they knew where he lived, worked, and spent his time," she noted aloud.

Devon nodded, but seemed to be fixating on something in the book. He flipped back a few pages, and then returned to this previous page. He did so numerous times before he looked up at her. "Perhaps it's not as bad as we initially feared."

"Really? How can you tell?" She didn't want to be hopeful, but she couldn't help but desperately cling to the possibility of a bright spot among all of the darkness.

"Upon further inspection, it appears all of these debts have been settled," he smiled, looking rather relieved himself.

"Oh?" Amelia was confused. "Money from my father?"

"No, I don't think so. It seems they were all paid off as part of a contractual agreement with a single investor. A Gabriel Desoto."

Amelia felt the color drain from her face as the room began to spin. Seeing her distress, Devon reached for her shoulders to steady her, leading her across the room to a chair at the desk. He sat down in the one next to her and leaned close.

"What is it, Amelia?"

"Gabriel Desoto. He's horrible. Ethan had mentioned business with him, but I never thought he would do so much. He must have been indebted to him for thousands."

Devon's face grew grave as he nodded with understanding as she relayed all she'd heard about the suspicious man from her conversations over the past several weeks.

"So Desoto is a definite suspect. If Ethan fell back on his word, Desoto would have had the motive and the means to harm him."

She nodded, but then felt her heart sink even further as she realized something else.

"He would have had the motive, yes, but so would someone else."

"Who?"

"Bennett."

"Bennett? That's preposterous!" Devon's friendly demeanor darkened as he sat back and folded his arms in disgust across his chest.

As she had done with her father, Amelia quickly explained in detail about Bennett's indignant tone towards his brother over the past days, and especially his adamant stance against any potential dealings with Gabriel Desoto.

"So, you see," she said, "if Ethan really owed Gabriel Desoto as much as you say, and Bennett found out, he would have been furious. Bennett knew Ethan had met with Desoto, but I doubt he realized how large the stakes were. If he found this ledger, and he confronted Ethan…"

Devon seemed to understand her thought process. "You're saying it could have been reactionary."

She hesitated, but then opted not to share her even darker thoughts that perhaps Bennett had planned the confrontation. Devon was faced with enough at the moment to have to consider a family member involved in premeditated murder. She nodded, and after a moment, he did the same.

"Yes, I can see how we need to consider that possibility. Either way, we need to get this ledger to the authorities immediately. It *must* have something to do with his murder."

He rose quickly and grabbed his jacket from the hat stand. She stood to do the same, and they stepped out again into the rain. Thankfully, her carriage driver had parked at a nearby stable, so Devon was able to quickly fetch him, and they rode together to the other end of town where Sheriff Hastings's office was located.

With Devon's help, Amelia explained what they had found and when the sheriff asked her pointed questions about what she knew and saw, she felt she had to be honest ad report everything. At the same time, she made it known that she sincerely hoped Bennett had nothing to do with it.

"You see, sir, Bennett has always been like a brother to me, and it would devastate my family if he was involved. I know I have to help by sharing all I know, or I wouldn't be doing Ethan justice. I simply couldn't live with that," she admitted quietly.

Sheriff Hastings shook Amelia and Devon's hands as they stood to leave.

"Thank you, Miss Sullivan. I give you my word that I will be extremely discreet and fair as I investigate. To be frank, I'd be surprised if Desoto didn't have something to do with this. He's bad news, as far as I've heard. And there's more than one man in this town that's lost a fortune to him over the past few years"—he held up the ledger—"but I've never held evidence like this against him, so for that I thank you."

Amelia nodded politely and left the building, already feeling a heavy burden lifted from her after sharing her suspicions with someone who could actually do something about it. Devon seemed to notice and said, "I see you're feeling better?"

She affirmed grimly, "Yes, thank you. As much as I can be, I suppose. I feel better for having pointed the investigation in some direction, but I hate the path it seems to be taking."

"I agree. I just pray Bennett isn't involved. That would kill May."

She agreed, but Amelia couldn't bring herself to reply for fear the investigation might not go in the direction she hoped, so she said nothing and instead stared out the window of the carriage as it hastened toward Morrow House where Devon would be staying while he was in town. Amelia bid farewell to him and instructed the coachman to help him in with his luggage.

"I'll walk the rest of the way home," she stated, and set off towards Sullivan's Pine via the river. It felt good to clear her thoughts and get a bit of fresh air. The rain had died down to a refreshing drizzle and she felt as if she was being cleansed from the blackness of the previous week. She walked slowly, stopping to admire the early Cherokee Rose blooms budding alongside the water's edge. She delicately ran her finger along the young foliage, remembering her many walks with Ethan along this seldom traversed path. Her heart hurt as she looked down at the riverbank. As if in a daydream, she could see Ethan clearly in front of her, laughing as they competitively chose rocks for an impromptu skipping tournament. Then he was suddenly right up next to her, presenting a wildflower bouquet to her on bended knee, his eyes scintillating with flirtatiousness. She closed her own eyes tightly, willing the memory to soothe her soul, but when they opened, he was gone, and the pain remained.

"Oh Ethan," she whispered. "Why did you have to leave me?"

Wiping her tears away, she quickened her pace and headed home. The house was quiet when she arrived, so she went to her room to change out of her muddy dress for dinner. Looking in the mirror, she was appalled by her dirt-stained appearance and rain-ruined hair, and she deduced a hot bath would help. She went down the hall to the bathroom and put wood on the stove to heat up water for a bath. Later, she sank into the hot water slowly, feeling its heat enter each pore. It did help her physical aches and tiredness dissipate, but her mind was just as weary when she emerged. She padded back down the hall to her room and began to freshen up, pulling out her most comfortable black bombazine dress from her wardrobe. She relished this chance for a few moments of solitude and decided to dress herself. A few moments later, while she was tying the last string on her bodice, Adele burst into her room.

"How could you, Amelia?" she cried.

"Adele? What is it?"

"They've arrested Bennett! They said he killed Ethan and that *you* gave them the evidence that proved it!"

Chapter 5

.

The overwhelming stench of sweat, human waste, and rotten food assaulted Amelia's nostrils as she stepped through the back door into a dark hallway lined with several jail cells. Ethan's funeral had been that morning, and Bennett's absence had been palpable. May hadn't the courage to visit him in prison in the days since his arrest. She was confused and sad, trying, physically, to survive the death of her twin. Now, seeing her other brother in prison for his murder was almost incomprehensible to her. Amelia offered to go in her place and visit Bennett, assuring May she would report back to her about how he was holding up.

Juliette fretted over Amelia's being seen in public so soon after burying her fiancé. "It's completely inappropriate, Amelia. You should be in complete seclusion for at least six weeks. Aside from the funeral and Sunday services at church, you shouldn't be going anywhere, let alone to a prison to see another man."

"Mother, it's not just another man. It's Ethan's brother. And I'm doing it for May. I feel a bit responsible for his incarceration. And I fully intend to be in complete mourning for at least six months, even though, if I may add, there is no set custom when one loses a person who was not actually her spouse. So, if I do leave the house, I'll do it in full mourning attire, dull silk and all. Lest you think I have any concern for what your stuffy friends may think of me, I don't. It's not for you or them; it's for Ethan," she asserted with finality and more sarcasm than she had intended.

Her mother silenced herself at that point, looking almost impressed to learn Amelia was so well educated on the customs of mourning. So it was that Amelia found herself itchingly sewn into a dull black dress, complete with the traditional crepe skirt that swished and crinkled with every step she took down the hallway of jail cells. She tried to keep her eyes focused straight ahead as she walked slowly past the first several cells, but she couldn't stop her eyes from staring at the men she passed. She recognized the local drunk, a thief her father had helped catch when he attempted to rob the mercantile, and a man who had been arrested for fighting with his cousin over a horse trade gone bad. In the last cell on the left, she saw Bennett, head hung low, huddled in the corner as far away from the other criminals as possible. He had only been there three days, but she could see the experience had already taken its toll. He looked broken.

What have I done?

Bennett raised his head as he heard her approaching. He looked relieved to see her when she stopped mid-step outside the cell door. She had expected him to be angry, hurt, or at least confused.

"Amelia!" His face shone happiness at her arrival, but his voice carried none of its usual buoyancy.

She forced a smile and nodded to Sheriff Hastings, who unlocked the cell door and allowed her to step inside before locking the door behind her. She turned to thank him and promised the visit would be brief.

"Take all the time you need, Miss Sullivan; he has nowhere to be." Returning her smile sympathetically, the sheriff turned and walked back to the front of the building.

Once they were alone, Amelia turned back to Bennett and gestured towards the bench along the wall of the cell. "May I sit?"

"Of course." Bennett stood and pointed to his chair. "I've found this seat to be more comfortable than the bench. Please, make yourself at home." Then, realizing the irony of his comment, he let out a chuckle. "If you can."

In spite of herself and the situation, she laughed loudly. Then, covering her mouth in embarrassment, she said, "I'm so sorry. I know there's nothing funny about this."

Bennett raised his hand in protest. "Amelia, it's fine. It's been a long few days for all of us. Please, tell me, how is May? I know all that has transpired must have really upset her."

Thankful to be of some help, Amelia gave him the full report. "She seems to be holding up well. The doctor said the baby is fine, and she is still able to eat and rest. We're all praying she will continue like this. She begged me to tell you not to worry about her. She knew you would. She wants you to focus on yourself."

Amelia continued by describing the funeral. It had been simple yet beautiful. Exactly as Ethan would have wanted. Knowing there would be scores of mourners, Amelia opted to have the funeral outside in the church yard in lieu of the small sanctuary. She took small comfort in the fact that the day itself was sunny, cool, and serene, with the sounds and scents of spring blossoming all around the cemetery. Reverend Twickingham quoted from the scripture she had selected out of Ethan's journals, and May and Devon both spoke warmly in memory of their brother and cousin. Bennett seemed pleased to hear that things went as well as possible.

Finding herself unable to continue with triviality, she paused, then hesitatingly asked, "How are you, Bennett?"

He smirked again. "I feel fine, although I'm sure I look ridiculous," he said as he instinctively ran his fingers through his dirty hair. "I'd give anything for a bath."

"I'm sure," Amelia nodded.

Bennett suddenly stood up and walked to the cell door. Resting his head between two rusted bars, he gazed out absentmindedly. He stood very still for several minutes, and Amelia patiently sat, waiting for him to speak.

Finally, he turned and looked back in her direction, but avoided her eyes. "Millie, what happened?" he asked in a near whisper.

It was Amelia's turn to drop her head. "I just... Oh...Bennett. I'm not quite sure," she began, blowing out the breath she didn't realize she'd been holding. "I thought the sheriff was looking into Gabriel Desoto, and the next thing I heard, they'd arrested you. Please understand—I never meant for this to happen to you, Bennett. I just couldn't keep what I knew a secret. Not if it meant finding out who killed Ethan."

"What do you mean, 'what you knew'?" he asked. "I didn't kill Ethan. Why would anything you had to tell the sheriff lead him to believe I did?"

"I saw you…" she stammered, "that night. I saw you walking into the woods down the path where Ethan…" She trailed off.

He began pacing quickly, agitated. "Fine, so I walked down that path when I left. So does everyone who works at your house. It could have been any of them!"

"But none of them were angry with him, Bennett, and you were. Everyone saw it. You were angry about the way he was handling your business. I heard you both arguing at your house a few weeks ago."

At first, he looked surprised as if he thought his long-standing disagreement with Ethan could have somehow been hidden from those around them. Then he shrugged.

"Of course I was angry with him! He was being erratic and making destructive decisions. He was planning to go into partnership with Gabriel Desoto. And he wouldn't listen to reason. I hated the thought of my family's hard-earned money being tainted by that snake. I did come back and talk to him that night when he left your house, but the only thing I wanted to do was convince him it would be a bad choice. I wouldn't kill him because of unethical business choices. He was my brother!"

Amelia was horrified; her worst fears and suspicions were now coming to fruition. "You came back?"

His face registered that she hadn't known that detail, and she detected a sudden sense of anguish. He continued. "Yes, I did. I'm certain that's why I'm in here—because I freely admitted it. I have nothing to hide about that night, Amelia. I've been completely truthful. I wanted to try one last time to stop Ethan from considering business with Desoto, but when he wouldn't listen, I left. That was the end of it. When I left him, I was angry. He was angry, too. But he was alive."

He turned away from her and walked to the other side of the cell near the door. His jaw was set sternly as he gazed out through the bars. She wanted so desperately to believe him because she could see that he was in deep pain, but he was still holding back and she knew she needed to confront him while he was being so apparently forthcoming.

"But he didn't just think about it, Bennett, he did it. Gabriel Desoto paid off all of his debts."

Bennett whipped around. "How did you know that?"

"Devon found the register in your office. Ethan was in debt to Desoto for thousands of dollars. It could have ruined your business. If you ask me, that's reason enough to kill him."

She knew as she said those words that there was still a big part of her that believed them. She was so emotionally conflicted; she had forgotten her initial feelings of remorse and now was starting to remember what had led her to share her suspicions with her father in the first place. Bennett had a lot to lose as a result of Ethan's poor business practices.

She pushed further. "You were so angry at dinner. Is that because you knew he had already signed over his debts to Desoto? So you argued, and you killed him?"

"What? No!" He shook his head furiously. "Amelia, think about what you're saying!"

She stepped forward and stood toe to toe with him. She needed answers. He couldn't know how confused and unsure she was. "I do know what I'm saying! For the first time in days, something makes sense. You lied! You stood in front of all of us and claimed to be angry about something which might happen in the future which, in reality, you knew had already happened! How do you explain that, Bennett?"

His jaw was clinched so tightly, she could see the blood coursing furiously through his temple. Finally, he collapsed onto the stool in the center of the room, rubbing the sweat from his forehead with the back of his hand. He looked defeated. "I can't," he conceded. "All I can tell you is that I didn't kill my brother."

"Well, I'm sorry to say that it will take more than that to convince me otherwise. Because at this point I don't see how anyone else could have done it. If the sheriff had enough evidence to arrest someone else, they would have."

They had reached an impasse, and they both knew it. Bennett's eyes glistened It struck her that even though they were the same warm eyes she had always known in her dearest friend, she now felt as if she were looking at a stranger, so weary was his countenance and broken his demeanor.

"Amelia, I know you are devastated by what has happened to Ethan. But I am, too. I want someone to blame as much as you do, but it's not me." He sighed and then continued. "The truth is, I lied about the status of Ethan's business with Desoto because I wanted to protect you and your family from finding out how stupid he'd been. I thought I could somehow get him out of it if I just convinced him in time. That's the only instance in which I haven't been completely truthful throughout this whole mess. But I can see that I won't convince you of that today, no matter what I say. I think it's time for you to leave."

Frustrated and emotionally spent, she nodded, and approached the cell door, gesturing to the guard. He came and inserted the brass key into the gate, taking her arm to lead her out into the aisle. She turned one last time to look at Bennett.

"I do hope that you're telling the truth, Bennett. Not only because you're my oldest friend, but to find out you killed Ethan would devastate May and Adele."

His eyes widened in surprise, and she realized that she'd slipped by mentioning her sister. She scolded herself. Adele would be so embarrassed to know she'd betrayed her feelings to Bennett, but she could do nothing about it now, so she said no more and turned to go back down the row of cells to exit the building.

Before leaving, she stopped to talk to the sheriff. "Sheriff Hastings, is it true you arrested Bennett because of the information I'd given you regarding Gabriel Desoto?"

He nodded. "That and the fact that the minute I approached him that same afternoon, Mr. Bennigan admitted to returning to your property and arguing with Ethan the night of his death. And there's no one to confirm his claim that he left Ethan alive. So, I'm obligated to follow the law. He had the means, motive, and opportunity to commit the crime, and I have no other suspects. Even though I would have loved to pin this on Gabriel Desoto, and believe me, I tried, it seems he's only connected to the Bennigan family business and not the murder."

Amelia was intrigued, so she pressed further. "May I ask how you know Desoto is not involved in the murder?"

Shrugging his shoulders, the sheriff pointed to a notebook on his desk on the other side of the room. "I interviewed several reliable local witnesses in the county who saw him that night at the tavern. He couldn't have been in two places at once."

Nodding, Amelia kept her thoughts to herself as she climbed back into her carriage to return home. The sheriff's last words had given her a glimmer of hope that maybe Bennett hadn't been the murderer.

Gabriel Desoto could have been at the tavern all night, she thought, *but it means that not only was he in the area, he was in the same town at the time. That can't be a coincidence. And who is to say that every filthy creature on his pay roll wasn't there with him?*

Her carriage halted, allowing a farmer leading cows to the auction house to cross in front of their path. As she sat waiting to continue on to Sullivan's Pine, a curious sensation began inching up her spine. Someone was watching her. She could feel it. Leaning forward, she cautiously glanced out the small window and immediately beheld a man she didn't recognize standing just steps from her carriage. The face was stunningly handsome, accentuated by an angular and fierce grin which she felt was specifically for her. The owner of that visage was tall, muscular, and impeccably dressed—a true Southern gentleman by all outward appearances—but something dark and nefarious drew her attention upward to meet his gaze. And there, she encountered pure darkness. His eyes, a piercing, hollow black, seemed to have nothing behind them—no compassion, no humanity, no humor—nothing. Although she'd never met him, his identity was no secret. It was Gabriel Desoto.

"Why is he here? Has he been following me?" she whispered to herself. It made her feel less alone to say it out loud.

The way Desoto had looked at her, that louring smile, made her even less sure about everything regarding the investigation. It seemed the sheriff was all but convinced that Bennett was the man and wouldn't listen to a woman's opinion either way; she knew that. It was just the way of things. If Bennett was really innocent, and Gabriel Desoto was responsible, she'd have to prove it herself. She just needed to figure out how.

The ride back to Sullivan's Pine felt extremely unsettling as she withdrew deeply into her thoughts. She yelped in surprise when the door opened at her front step.

"I'm sorry, Miss," the sweet, old coachman, Jeffrey, apologized, taking off his hat and bowing.

Amelia shook her head and laughed nervously. "No need, Jeffrey. I just wasn't paying attention."

She accepted his hand and stepped down from the carriage. As she did, she glanced up at her house. She so infrequently entered through the front that she often forgot how beautifully grand a structure it was—one of the biggest houses in the county, and without doubt the most extravagant home in Moon Springs. She remembered with fondness the many county-wide debutante balls, coming-out parties, and other major social events that had been held there over the years.

Although a tomboyish child, she had loved, gazing out the window from her room at the elegant ladies who arrived to waltz until dawn. Of course, when she had been a little girl, she'd always been sent to bed before the real fun began, but by the time she was old enough to attend, she hadn't the time to watch the excitement of the arrivals as she was vigorously engaged assisting her mother in the role of hostess. Even if the frills and glamour of the galas hadn't fulfilled her girlhood fantasies as they did for other young ladies her age, Amelia didn't fail to recognize the importance of such occasions. A girl's life could change forever at one of those parties. She could meet the beau of her dreams. *Or at least her mother's*, Amelia smiled to herself.

She started to walk up the stairs towards her front door when a sudden notion yanked her back. She turned and looked back down the long drive towards the front gate, lined with rows of welcoming cherry blossom trees, and back again towards her house. It was a stretch of an idea, and she certainly couldn't do it alone, but it just might work, Amelia surmised as she quickly entered the grand hallway and began shouting for Adele.

Juliette threw open the parlor door and entered the hall with a horrified look on her face.

"What is it, Amelia? Are you all right?"

Amelia embarrassingly covered her mouth and curtseyed out of obligatory habit to her mother's Old Country traditional demands. "I'm so sorry to shout, Mother. I'm fine. I'm just looking for Adele."

"Young lady, I know we've been through a great deal this past week, but there is no need to revert to barbarianism. Heavens!" Juliette whirled around, the taffeta and crinoline train rustling behind her as she huffed back to her station in the parlor.

"Yes, ma'am." Amelia nodded to her mother's back.

"You did it this time, Amelia," Adele laughed as she descended the stairs from the shadows of the landing to greet her sister.

"Oh, good, you heard me!"

"The entire house heard you, and quite possibly that old man who lives on the other side of the river," Adele joked.

It was so good to see Adele smile, even if the moment was brief. Amelia took her by the hand and walked into their father's study. She slid the door closed behind them. Adele, obviously curious, raised an eyebrow at Amelia's mysterious behavior.

"What's going on, Millie?"

"I've been to see Bennett."

Adele's expression abruptly shifted, changing from curiosity to urgent angst. She grabbed both of Amelia's hands and led her to sit down on the end of the leather chaise situated farthest from the door so that they would not be overheard.

"I didn't know you were going to see Bennett," Adele said.

"I wanted him to hear about the funeral," Amelia began. "I also wanted to make sure he was doing all right."

"And?" Adele pleaded.

Amelia patted her sister's hands in a vain attempt to assuage her concern. "He seems to be holding his own, although he misses the comforts of home."

Adele looked towards town out the window, as if she could transport herself to the jail to be sure Amelia spoke the truth. Then she turned back to her sister. "Why does this need to be such a secret?"

"Because I don't want anyone to overhear and worry unnecessarily, but something happened on the way home. As I was riding home in the carriage I saw Gabriel Desoto standing on the street across from the jail, as if he was monitoring the goings and comings of everyone who went inside."

"Why would he even be there?"

"I don't know, unless he has someone on his payroll on the inside."

Adele's eyes widened. "You don't think they'll harm him, do you?"

Amelia considered this for a moment, and then shook her head. "No, I don't. As long as Bennett stays in jail, Desoto can continue to do whatever he wants. He wouldn't risk creating a scene by ordering someone to hurt Bennett. Then it would be obvious Bennett is innocent."

"Is that what you think now, that he's innocent?" Adele sounded so hopeful.

Amelia sighed. "I don't know what I think, Adele. I can't deny what I saw the night Ethan died. But I also can't ignore the upright man I know Bennett to be. And seeing Desoto just now, I'm just so unsure of everything. There is something very dark about that man." She described the brief encounter.

Adele gasped and covered her mouth. "Oh, he sounds terrible!" she exclaimed.

Amelia frowned, thinking for a moment. "Terrible, yes. But really, he looked very much like a normal well-bred gentleman—handsome, poised, finely dressed. If I hadn't known who he was, I would have thought nothing of it at first glance, until I looked into his eyes and saw nothing but contempt."

Adele shivered. "Well, I think he sounds awful. I hope I never have to meet him."

Amelia shook her head. "But you see, we do need to see him. In fact, we need to see him often for my plan to work."

"What plan?"

"I plan to get close to him to tear down his defenses and get him to confess that he had Ethan killed. Because now that I've seen him and looked into those horrible eyes, I am convinced that it is him who is guilty of Ethan's murder, not Bennett."

Amelia looked away guiltily and waited patiently for Adele to begin scolding her, reminding her that Bennett was in this mess in the first place thanks to her. But she didn't.

"How are you going to get close to him, Amelia? You're in mourning! You can't very well socialize intimately with another man so soon after Ethan's death. Even if you weren't yet his wife, you do owe him that."

"Of course! No, I will continue on in mourning, not only because society requires it but also my soul is just so weary still. To be truthful though, I'm sure mourning is the opposite of what Ethan would have wanted. But, because he was never actually my husband, not everyone in the family needs to be in mourning." She searched her sister's eyes for a sign of comprehension of her intent. Finding none, she spoke each word deliberately. "I'm in mourning, Adele, but you're not."

Adele was horrified. "Oh, Amelia, you can't mean you want me to get him to confess? I could never get close to a man as evil as him. I don't have it in me to be so deceitful. And what if Bennett heard? What would he think of me?"

Again, Amelia declined to indicate Bennett's awareness of Adele's feelings, and instead focused on the task at hand. "Adele, think of it as doing it *for* Bennett. I truly believe this is the only way to get him released from prison. As of now, Sheriff Hastings thinks he is the guilty party. The only way to free Bennett is to prove that someone else is responsible. I believe that to be Gabriel Desoto. I think he hired someone to murder Ethan. He is behind it somehow."

Adele weighed Amelia's words carefully. "I don't know, Amelia. It makes sense, but I'd have to lie to him, and you know I'm a terrible liar!"

She has me there, Amelia thought. Adele always showed her feelings. But she needed her sister's help, so she encouraged her otherwise. It was her only hope.

"You can do this, Adele. And we can be careful. You'll never be in danger. I think Desoto thinks I blame Bennett, so he may let his guard down. If we work our connections just right, we may be able to get him to confess before he even realizes what's happening."

"And how in the world would I go about meeting him, anyway?" Adele demanded.

"At the Debutante Ball,"Amelia proudly announced, expecting her sister to be in awe of her brilliance.

"But I just heard Mother say the ball has been cancelled out of respect for you and May, and in light of Bennett's current…circumstances," Adele finished with disdain.

"I can take care of that. I'll just tell Mother I need something to distract me. Planning a formal ball will give me the chance to do that. She'll be so delighted I want to participate in such a ladylike event, she'll have to reinstate it!"

"But you can't attend a ball while in mourning, Amelia."

"I won't attend. I'll stay in my room. Anyway, that will give me a chance to keep an eye on things from afar and make sure you stay safe."

At the mention of her safety, Adele eyed the door as if suddenly looking for an escape route. "Oh dear, I hadn't even thought of it as being dangerous. I was just worried about Bennett finding out."

Amelia reassured her. "You'll be perfectly safe. You'll never be alone since it's a ball, and if all goes well, and you establish a good *rapport* with Gabriel, then we'll be sure to set up your future meetings in public. Plus, I can let Devon in our plans so that he will know to keep an extra eye out for you at the ball. He has promised to stay several more weeks to help May get the family business affairs sorted out."

"Devon? Can we trust him?"

"Please, don't worry.He is completely trustworthy."

"I just have one more question," Adele said.

"What's that?"

"How are you sure Gabriel Desoto will even attend the ball? He's never been to anything around here before."

"We're the wealthiest family in the county, Adele. Father is one of the only people not already indebted to him. He'll try to change that, undoubtedly, and will need an opportunity such as this to approach Father. Trust me; he'll be there."

Chapter 6

Amelia was quite sure she'd never seen so much vibrantly colored and expertly hung tulle, silk, and satin in all her life as she did in her very own house in the hours leading up to the ball. Just when she'd thought they were done with the decorations and place settings, another clerk from the mercantile would come trudging up the front steps with a new box of china to display or a bolt of fabric to drape over the already opulent window dressings in the hall and ballroom.

Opening up the Debutante Ball to the entire county had ensured a completely full ballroom of no less than a hundred attendees and a totally overwhelmed Juliette. Mrs. Sullivan had spent every waking minute of the previous five weeks planning the affair. As prepared as Amelia had been for a battle with her mother over the recent cancellation of the ball, she was surprised at how quickly she convinced her otherwise. In fact, Juliette seemed almost glad to have something to do with her nervous energy.

God love her, Amelia thought, as she watched her mother flutter around the kitchen, confirming last-minute details, *but she is just too elegant for a life of mourning.*

Amelia was, herself, still extremely comfortable in her full mourning attire and mindset. These past weeks had allowed her a chance to process the death of Ethan while also giving her an outlet for her anxiety by assisting her mother in planning the ball.

To her surprise, grief was *not* unproductive. When the world had finally stopped spinning around her, she'd been able to at least acknowledge the fact that Ethan wouldn't be coming back. Although she knew it would be eons, if ever, before she came to a point of acceptance, and she would probably never stop grieving for him, throwing her efforts into something productive was helpful, albeit temporary.

Her first priority after Juliette had agreed to reinstate the ball was to write to Bennett. She had to choose her words carefully, especially where Adele was concerned, but she felt she needed him to know she believed him to be innocent—and that she was doing everything possible to get him out of prison and bring Ethan's real killer to justice. She informed him that she'd seen Gabriel Desoto in town after visiting him, and that she was absolutely positive Desoto was responsible for Ethan's death. She knew a meager letter wouldn't reverse the fact that Bennett was in prison because of her, but she hoped it would at least comfort him to know his family would not rest until he was free.

Sheriff Hastings had promised to personally deliver the letter himself to Bennett so she wouldn't have to worry that Desoto or any of his minions would intercept it. The sheriff also assured her that although he still hadn't found any evidence against Desoto, he also hadn't found anything more to add to the state's case against Bennett either—not from his own testimony, witness statements, or the Bennigan business records. Amelia clung to a sliver of hope that something would turn up to implicate someone.

So far, her plan had worked with flawless perfection. Among the scores of response cards for the ball had been one signed "Gabriel James Desoto." She'd almost been disappointed that she hadn't had to wait in suspense to see if he would take her bait once her mother had his personalized invitation delivered to the small inn where he'd been staying in the village.

Unsurprisingly, the biggest obstacle Amelia had faced was convincing her parents to invite Desoto to the ball, especially since she had no intention of revealing her plan to them. Her father would lock her in her room and throw away the key if he knew what she and Adele intended to do.

"There's no chance on God's green earth that I will have that man in my house!" her father had shouted when she had suggested it over dinner one night.

Her mother's response had been less boisterous but still firm.

"Amelia," she'd said, placing her napkin in her lap after dabbing away some crumbs, "he is such a controversial character. I can't see what good would come from having him, and there are many benefits to leaving him out. He doesn't even live here, so we're certainly not obligated to extend an invitation."

Thankfully, Amelia had prepared herself for this reaction from both of her parents, so had laid out her readied arguments methodically.

"On the contrary, Mother. If I may, I think there is much to gain from inviting Mr. Desoto to the ball. For one, it shows him we will not be intimidated as a family after Ethan's death. If Ethan was indebted to him for as much as Devon and Bennett claim he was, he may try to manipulate us into paying it off and going on the offense from the start would deter him."

Amelia still hadn't revealed to her father that she knew he had been financially supporting Ethan during the past year. Out of respect for Ethan's and the Sullivan name, she had decided there was no need to do so, at least at this point.

"Besides," she'd continued, "whether we like it or not, and whether his methods are pure or not, he is one of the wealthiest individuals in the state. And, as we all know, wealth brings power—politically, socially, and economically. We wouldn't want him to be offended by not receiving an invitation. So far, he has left Sullivan's Mercantile out of his grasp, and we need to keep it that way."

"As if I would ever do any business with the likes of him," Michael had grumbled, his Irish temper flaring.

"Of course not, Papa, but he is so influential, he could steer business away from you without ever setting foot in the mercantile, and he could do it easily."

Her father's face fell, and at that moment she knew she had him. After sitting in defiant silence for a few more seconds, he had begrudgingly agreed, and Juliette sent the invitation to Desoto the next morning.

Amelia's next move was securing Devon's assistance. That part had been easy. The more she reacquainted herself with Devon, the more she saw how much of the Bennigan spirit he had. He was a man intrigued by an adventure, much as Ethan had been. What he had on his side that Ethan had lacked was the willpower to keep it in check. It was the perfect balance and exactly what she needed in an ally at this moment.

She invited Devon over for dinner one late April evening and afterwards suggested they take a walk in the gardens. She caught her mother raising an eyebrow at her disapprovingly, so Amelia asked Adele if she'd like to join them.

The evening sun was a welcome change to the rainy spring days they'd been suffering through of late, so Adele eagerly agreed, and the trio headed out through the dining room doors onto the patio. Attempting to look innocently engaged in lighthearted conversation in case her mother was still keeping track of them from the window, Amelia linked arms with Adele and pretended to admire the plethora of the latest spring blooms. As she bent to inhale the soothing scent of a hyacinth peeking out from around a stone bench in the main garden, she divulged her plan to Devon.

They casually meandered to each section of the garden and then proceed to the wild azalea trail leading towards the creek. Devon listened intently while Amelia laid out every detail she had devised up to this point. When she was finished, he seemed intrigued and more than a little impressed that she'd managed to get her mother to invite Desoto without more of a fight.

"Brilliant," he'd said. "What can I do to help?"

"Well," Amelia gestured to Adele, "most importantly, don't let her leave your sight on the night of the ball. I can't see how he could possibly figure out what I am doing, but if, for some reason, he does, I don't want Adele to be alone with Desoto where he could cause her harm."

"Done," he'd agreed. "But what about you? It might look a bit ambitious if I'm trying to entertain two ladies at the same ball, not that I couldn't handle it."

"You flatter yourself, Mr. Bennigan," Amelia smirked.

He'd laughed, and Amelia felt her heart beat a bit faster when she again saw the resemblance to Ethan. She pushed the thought away quickly. She had no time for the confusion it elicited.

"I think that if you could work to gain his confidence yourself, perhaps by intimating that you are the one organizing Ethan's papers and accounts after his death, Desoto's curiosity will be piqued, and he might actually try to engage you in a conversation regarding any outstanding debts Ethan may have owed him to see if there had been a plan in place to ensure they were paid back. Honestly, I hope he does exactly that. Then we could determine how much motive he would have had to kill Ethan."

Devon had nodded in understanding.

"Oh, and one more thing," Amelia concluded, stopping to inspect a light pink hydrangea she had not seen before. "Make sure he is fully aware that May has absolutely no input or holding in the Bennigan finances. I want her left completely out of this. She is upset enough with Ethan being murdered and Bennett in jail. It would ruin her to know that Ethan had actually gotten in so deeply with Desoto."

On that point, Adele and Devon enthusiastically agreed.

The first carriage rolled up to the front door at precisely six o'clock, per her mother's invitations.

Michael instructed Nancy and Fanny to notify the rest of the family that it was time to receive their guests. Nancy, who had recovered from her emotional trauma on the night of the murder, had begged to return to the fair and generous employ of the Sullivan family. This was her first evening back at the house.

Amelia was in her room, pinning back the last few tendrils that stubbornly refused to stay in place, when she heard a light tapping at her door.

"Come in."

The door pushed open, and her mother stepped into the room. Juliette tilted her head for a moment, sizing up her daughter, then crossed the room and picked up some more pins from the bureau and stood behind Amelia, pushing one in here, one in there.

Her mother hadn't done her hair in years, but Amelia didn't mind. It was endearing. She relaxed her arms down to her side, and let Juliette take over. They remained in contented silence while Juliette worked on her coiffure. When she was finished pinning, Juliette continued gently smoothing back pieces of Amelia's hair, more out of affection than necessity.

"Amelia," she finally said. "You've done a wonderful job helping me plan the ball."

"Thank you, Mother. I rather enjoyed it, surprisingly."

And she had—even the parts that had nothing to do with luring in Desoto. She had genuinely enjoyed working alongside her mother these past several weeks, which was a rarity since they differed so much in nature.

"Yes, well, it's going to be absolutely beautiful, and I think everyone will have a lovely time. The role of Debutante may seem silly to some, but there's much to be learned from the experience, including proper manners and poise. I can think of many young ladies who met their future husbands at the galas we've hosted before."

Amelia nodded. "Sally O'Malley, to name one."

"Yes, and three years ago there was Lydia Stark who met that doctor she married when he was visiting his brother in town."

"I'd forgotten about them." Amelia paused, deciding to play along. "Maybe Adele will meet someone tonight. Wouldn't that be something?"

Juliette frowned. "Perhaps. I do hope she ends up with a smart match. Lord knows she's accustomed to so much; I'm sure I'm partly to blame, but she'll be a tough one to please for a man. She's too much like your aunt."

"I think you're underestimating Adele. She'd absolutely choose love over money if it came down to it."

"Well, for her sake, and his, I hope it ends up being both," her mother joked. "Regardless, this will be a wonderful evening. You've thought of everything —designed the best menu with the chef, made sure everyone under creation was invited. I'm quite proud. I think it's perfectly fine for you stay up here rather than join us downstairs."

Amelia looked at her mother's reflection in the small vanity mirror and frowned. "I'm not sure I understand."

She could see her mother was trying to be tactful. "I'm worried about you, Millie. I'm afraid we've indulged you too much since Ethan died by letting you stay so busy that you've not yet had a chance to truly grieve his loss. I would be doing you a disservice as your mother if I didn't encourage you to do that."

"I'm grieving in my own way. If I thought it would be helpful to cry the day away, I'd do it. I just see no use in that."

"As long as you're sure you're not simply avoiding it, because if you are, you won't ever begin to heal."

"Honestly, I don't know that I want to heal, Mother."

Juliette turned Amelia's shoulders towards her so she could look into her face.

"*Ma fille*, that would be doing yourself—and Ethan—a serious disservice. He would want differently for you. I think you know that."

She said nothing else, just leaned over and kissed Amelia's hair gently, then turned to leave the room. Amelia stood to follow her, but she stopped instead to watch her mother walk away. She was touched by her compassion yet wondered how much of Juliette's concern stemmed from a drive to keep up appearances.

Sensing her daughter's eyes on her back, Juliette turned around on the landing to the stairs, her yellow silk gown elegantly brushing the floor.

"Are you coming, dear?"

Amelia nodded. "Yes, ma'am. It's just that you look so beautiful, and I look...horrendous."

"Thank you, *ma fafille*," her mother said, smiling gracefully, "and you look beautiful, too."

Amelia laughed. It was practically impossible to look anything but horrid in mourning attire, but since she was now out of full mourning, she had decided to wear a black gown made of an almost reflective satin. Her full skirt swirled underneath her whenever she turned, and even though it was all black, it was still very flattering. They went down the stairs together and took their positions in the hall to wait for Michael and Adele.

Glancing out the front window to the large, welcoming porch at the head of the house, Juliette turned back. "I believe your Aunt Louisa and Uncle Patrick are the first arrivals."

"Oh good!" Amelia said. She was grateful to be able to spend a moment chatting with her aunt before other guests arrived and her attention was diverted elsewhere.

"My sister?" Michael teased as he reached the bottom stair, Adele on his arm. "Make her wait out there for the real guests to arrive!"

"Adele, dear, you look magnificent!" Juliette cooed.

"Thank you, Mother," Adele curtseyed, her blonde hair pinned into a delicate chignon at her neck which just grazed the high back of her bright pink gown that was expertly enhanced with lace over the entire dress.

The front door swung open, and Samuel, May, Louisa, and Patrick all entered amidst jovial conversation.

"Amelia!" Louisa quickly stepped forward to embrace her niece tightly. "How are you holding up, dear?"

"As well as can be expected, I think. You look lovely, as usual." Amelia squeezed her hand back reassuringly.

Louisa gleefully took a step back and twirled so they could all admire the full effect of her dress. The dark green satin was set off brilliantly by her red hair, which was pulled halfway back with a diamond-studded hairpin.

"Thank you! It *is* lovely, isn't it? Satin is my newfound love. I used to fear it would be too warm for this hot Georgia air, but it really is comfortable, and thankfully looks amazing on everyone!" she declared.

"Of course, there is never any mention of the price," Patrick smiled.

"Oh, Patrick," Louisa said, poking him lovingly. "You would have me in a burlap sack if we were going to base my clothing choices on price!"

They both laughed as Patrick took her hand and proceeded to enter the ballroom. The small orchestra Amelia had hired began to play the prelude on her signal. Amelia turned to Adele and motioned for her to stand beside her.

In a hushed voice, she asked, "Are you ready?"

Adele nodded nervously. "I think so. You're sure Devon will be able to stay close enough without its being obvious?"

Amelia reassured her. "Yes. He is going to pretend he is vying for your attention, which would give him a perfectly good reason to stay close, even frustratingly so. You just need to make sure it is obvious you don't return his admiration beyond friendship, and solely focus your efforts on Gabriel."

"Oh wonderful," Adele huffed. "Two suitors at the same ball and neither of them is the one I really want."

Proud of her sister's newfound abilities to be forthcoming with her feelings, Amelia gave her a little hug. "Don't worry. Bennett knows all about this."

"It's not him I worry about. It's everyone else in the county. You know they will talk!"

Scolding herself, Amelia covered her hand with her mouth. She had completely neglected to take into account the effect her plan could have on Adele's reputation. How could she have been so selfish? "Oh, Adele!" she gasped. "I hadn't thought of that! It's not too late to call the whole thing off. I can't ask you to do anything that would damage your reputation."

It was Adele's turn to be reassuring. She linked her arm with her sister's and gently patted it. "I'm sorry, Amelia. I shouldn't have even said anything. I'm sure I'm just nervous. This is so unlike anything I've ever done. If we can catch Desoto, the truth will come out eventually, so I will only have to live with the gossip for a short while, if at all. It's a small sacrifice if it means getting Bennett out of prison and helping you find Ethan's killer. We will continue as planned." Adele straightened up and smiled dutifully as the first true guests arrived through the front door.

Amelia took a step back to join her mother and father in the receiving line. Her plan was to receive the guests, make sure Desoto met Adele, and then return to her room for the evening. As much as she felt she was ready for some societal interactions, she wasn't up for dancing and dinner conversations just yet—and certainly not in the same room as Gabriel Desoto.

She was grateful to see familiar faces, and everyone was genuinely gracious in their condolences over the loss of Ethan, and very complimentary on the evening's ambiance. Amelia was pleased that everything was going so well, even though she'd planned the event with ulterior motives. The time in the receiving line passed quickly, and she found herself a less apprehensive and almost forgetting her reasons for having this gathering. She discreetly turned to watch the guests mingling and occasionally glanced at the couples dancing in the ballroom as they waited for the supper trays to be laid out. She noticed the flushed faces of the debutantes holding the arms of the dashing young escorts they'd arrived with. They looked so happy and blissfully unaware of anything besides that very moment. She envied them. She wondered if some day she would be able to return to normalcy like that—but she held out little hope. Her sadness pervaded her being, and she felt empty inside as if she could never be filled with the joy of loving again.

Someone's hand on her shoulder stirred her from her thoughts. She turned to look back and was relieved to find it was Devon. He looked remarkably handsome with his hair swept back from his face, exposing his strong brow. Smiling down at her warmly, he took her hand in his and kissed it cordially. She felt heat rise into her face. No other man's lips had touched her skin since she'd been in Ethan's arms. She shuddered as she looked up at Devon and said *hello*. She wished she could pull him aside and speak privately about their plan, but she knew that would look and feel inappropriate, so she simply said, "I hope you came prepared for an intriguing evening, Devon. Adele is looking lovely tonight, isn't she?"

Taking his cue, Devon turned his attention to Adele and bowed courteously. "Good evening, Adele."

Adele returned his bow with a curtsey and gestured to the ballroom. "Please head on in to the ballroom, Devon. I know May and Samuel will be happy to see you! I'll be sure to join you all later."

He nodded and said, "I do hope you'll consider saving me a dance, Adele."

Hesitating, Adele glanced sideways at Amelia who nodded slightly. It would be good for them to have a chance to debrief if necessary. "Of course. It would be my pleasure."

He bowed once again to both of them and turned to walk into the other room to find his cousin and her husband. Amelia saw the group meet close to the punch table. May did seem pleased to see Devon. Having him in town helping her sort through Ethan and Bennett's business had given her the familial support she desperately needed in her time of grief.

Amelia glanced at the clock in the hall. The ball had officially started more than thirty minutes ago. The guest arrivals had trickled down next to nothing, and there was still no sign of Desoto. She began to wonder if her plan had been foiled when she saw one last carriage coming down the lane. Holding her breath in anticipation, she let it out in a frustrated huff when she saw the door open to reveal Nellie O'Malley and her husband, Brian. She tried to hide disappointment as they rushed in apologetically.

"Juliette, dear, we're so sorry to be late. Our carriage wheel broke this afternoon, and we had to wait for a replacement to be delivered from town." Nellie kissed Juliette's cheeks and then breezed into the ballroom as quickly as she had blown into the house.

"Well, Amelia, I think we are through receiving guests. If you'll excuse me, I will join your father in the ballroom." Her mother hugged her warmly.

"That's fine, Mother. I'll see you tomorrow. Please, do enjoy yourself. Everything looks beautiful."

"I couldn't have done it without you, dear." Her mother smiled and then left to join her guests.

Sighing in defeat, Amelia decided to sneak into the kitchen, grab a basket of party food, take it to her room. She had smelled the fragrance of quail roasting all afternoon and just had to have a bite. Once in the kitchen, she found their cook, Eleanor, and other kitchen staff they'd hired for the evening, hard at work assisting the French chef her mother had hired solely for this event.

Amelia stood in the doorway for several minutes, watching a masterpiece of cuisine come together in perfect harmony. Chef Michel Baudin was truly an artist at his craft. In one corner, he had Eleanor wrapping the fresh oysters from Savannah in succulent strips of bacon. One of the hired sous chefs was across the room chopping fresh vegetables that would be paired with an assortment of hard and soft cheeses and served to the guests while they waited for the main course. Amelia watched the man's wrists flex expertly as he diced, his dark skin contrasting with the ivory of the cutting board.

Chef Baudin had been thrilled to learn the existence of a local farmer in the family and had ordered a large supply of cabbages from Louisa and Patrick. He boiled, then rolled and stuffed them with a goat's cheese, garlic, and potato mash. Amelia had seen how proud Patrick had been when he'd heard the news.

"See, Louisa? Even the fancy French chef knows that good Southern farmers are a valuable asset to our culture," he'd proudly stated.

Louisa patted him on the arm. "Of course, darling. I'm so happy we can be of use to him!"

And they were. Nearly every fresh produce item for the entire ball had been supplied by the O'Brien plantation, from the vegetables to the peaches used in the cobbler being served in hundreds of individual silver bowls for dessert. Amelia felt a surge of pride as she looked around the kitchen at the culmination of weeks of planning. The food was going to be superb, the ballroom was exquisite, and the only thing missing was Ethan.

As she savored the mixture of brine of the oysters and richness of the uncured bacon, she mused about how interested he would have been in the process of getting the oysters there that day. Chef Boudin had made sure to order them ahead of time and arrange for Jeffrey to drive to the nearest railroad town to spend the night before the ball so he would be there to meet the train coming from Savannah as soon as possible. The oysters had been loaded into the back of the Sullivan Mercantile icebox wagon and driven the additional hour back to Moon Springs. They were certainly safe to eat and incredibly tasty, but there was always the unknown danger in transporting perishable foodstuffs if Jeffrey ran into trouble en route.

If he was here, Amelia smiled to herself, *Ethan would have used the promise of fresher fish as a platform to promote his dreams of bringing a railroad to town.* She loved good seafood and had never even thought of the possibilities of more access to it with the addition of the railroad.

Eleanor helped Amelia gather a small basket of samplings to take to her room, and then Amelia went to offer her congratulations to the chef on his accomplishments of the evening.

He returned her gratitude with a jolly laugh and handshake. "It has been my pleasure, *mademoiselle.* America has proven to be full of culinary possibilities."

Amelia was glad to hear it. "Oh, well then perhaps you should consider staying and opening a restaurant, perhaps in Charleston or Savannah? I'm sure it would be a great success!"

He thanked her for the suggestion and then returned to his coordination of the evening. Amelia felt strangely productive as she left the kitchen and headed back out into the hallway for one last glimpse of the ball before heading to her room. She stood back behind the doorframe and quietly observed. The women were all spectacular and the men handsome in their tailored suits. Everyone seemed to be having a wonderful time. Satisfied, she turned towards the staircase but stumbled clumsily when she collided with a tall body in a dark navy suit.

"I'm sorry. Please excuse me," she apologized, bowing her head to curtsey and try to move out of the way, but the guest grabbed her elbow, jerking her to a halt.

"It is I who should be making the apologies, Miss Sullivan, along with my condolences, I understand," answered a frighteningly smooth voice.

Amelia forgot her manners, her eyes bolting upright to stare into the same hauntingly handsome face she'd seen from the window of her carriage weeks before. He was here.

Trying desperately to regain her composure, she feigned a puzzled expression dressed with a smile any hostess would be proud of and said, "I'm afraid I haven't had the pleasure, sir. I'm Amelia Sullivan; this is my parents' home. I do hope you will enjoy yourself!"

"I'm Gabriel Desoto." He peered down at her suspiciously. "But I suspect you already knew that, didn't you?"

He seemed to stare right through her into the depths of her soul, and she shuddered. *He can't know I suspect him of anything,* she reminded herself and straightened up to shake his hand.

"Mr. Desoto! Of course! Yes, Ethan always spoke so highly of you and your fascinating plans for our area. I am pleased to finally meet you." She paused, then added, "And thank you kindly for your sincere thoughts on the loss of Ethan." Her lips trembled on her last words— " I loved him dearly."

She gestured into the ballroom. "Please, do go on in and enjoy yourself. I believe they're preparing to serve the main course soon. I would hate for you to miss out on such a delightful culinary experience."

He looked surprised as she began to step towards the hallway. "You won't be joining the festivities, Miss Sullivan?"

She turned back around to answer him.

"No. I'm still deeply grieving the loss of Ethan, and even if it were socially acceptable, I'm afraid my heart wouldn't be in it. So, if you'll excuse me, I will take my leave for the evening."

She moved to the side to pass him when she felt his hand firmly grab her shoulder. Her first instinct was to slap his arm away, but she maintained her composure and met his intense gaze with one of her own. "Pardon me, but did you lose your footing?" she smiled. "This old house does tend to be unstable at this time of year with the weather warping the wooden floors so often."

"No, I'm actually quite steady on my feet, Miss Sullivan," he sneered. "I do, however, need to make something quite clear." He tightened his grip, and Amelia winced under the pressure. Her common sense told her he wouldn't dare hurt her with hundreds of people just feet away, but her fear was getting the better of her. She looked up helplessly, waiting for him to continue.

He bent his head to hers, and his voice dropped to a hoarse whisper. "I know you're aware that Ethan and I did some business together. And I know I have a reputation that precedes me, in spite of my best efforts to remain in everyone's good graces. But I need you to understand that my business with your former fiancé was legitimate, legal, and binding. When he died he owed me a large sum of money. And I intend to be repaid. His status as a person, living or dead, does not exclude him from paying me what I'm owed, with interest, as agreed. It's why I'm still here in this forsaken county instead of in the city where I belong. So," he paused, "if you're ready to be rid of me, you'll help me find my money. Otherwise, you should prepare to see me again."

Her fear was quickly displaced by anger. She forgot all social graces, violently wrenched her hand from his grasp, and took two steps backwards to even the playing field. Then she crossed her arms and said, "I'm sorry, Mr. Desoto. I'm not sure where you're from or how you were raised, but I can tell you two things. The first is that no real gentleman alive would ever talk to a lady like that, so I suggest you adjust your demeanor before one of *them* decides to escort you out against your will before you get to dance one waltz. And, secondly, around here if you're not married to someone, you have no access to their money, so I'm afraid you're on your own in your search for your 'repayment,' as you call it. I can't help you, and even if

I could, from what I've seen tonight, I would choose otherwise."

His comely face twisted into an evil grin, similar to the one he had sported the first time she'd laid eyes on him, and he stepped towards her once again. She grabbed the hem of her skirt to attempt a retreat up the stairs when Devon abruptly emerged from the ballroom and stepped right in front of Amelia, so near to her that caught the short of her petticoat under his boot as he towered over her.

"I'm sorry to interrupt, but, Amelia, your mother was searching for her yellow handkerchief and wondered if you might fetch it from her room for her."

Amelia was confused. Her mother didn't own a yellow handkerchief. But Devon had already changed the subject by introducing himself to Desoto. When Gabriel heard who he was, his eyes gleamed with triumph. He'd found the man who would help him retrieve his money—or so he thought. Amelia tried to think of a way she could secretly warn Devon about how dark their conversation had quickly turned, but he turned to her first and pointed upstairs.

"Amelia, would you be so kind?"

Realizing he was giving her a chance to escape, she nodded and turned briefly back to Gabriel. "I should look for my mother's kerchief. It was a pleasure meeting you, Mr. Desoto. Please, enjoy your evening."

Without waiting for a reply, Amelia turned and raced up the stairs and broke into a run when she was out of sight. She didn't even take a breath until she was in her room, and the door was locked behind her. Sinking to the floor, her back against the door, she could feel her heart pounding wildly, and she sat there for several minutes trying to calm down.

When she was sure dinner would be over and everyone would be engulfed in the post-meal dancing, Amelia tiptoed down the servant staircase that led into the kitchen. She pushed open the large wooden door a crack and peered through. The room was deserted, so she quickly crossed to the steps leading up into the garden and closed the door quietly behind her. She could hear the kitchen staff enjoying their own celebratory occasion around the back of the house, no doubt thrilled their services were no longer required. Careful to not make her presence known, she took off her shoes and tiptoed in bare feet around to the front of the house where she would be able to peer into the windows of the ballroom.

When she reached the point where there were no more tall shrubs blocking her from view, she threw decorum to the wind, resigning herself to the fact that her dress would likely not survive the evening, and fell to her knees to crawl under the first few sets of windows until she reached the corner window. From there, she would be able to look in the room but would be covered by the large coat rack that hung in front, ensuring she would not be seen.

She could have waited until the ball was over to get a full report from Adele, as had been their original intent, but her encounter with Gabriel had so shaken her resolve that she had the upper hand in the situation, and she felt an urgency to see with her own eyes that things were going according to plan. Plus, she needed to see for herself that her sister was being watched over by Devon now that she had seen Desoto's true colors.

She carefully raised her head high enough to be able to see into the room, her eyes just above the stone sill. As she suspected, nearly everyone was out on the dance floor. The room was a crowded jumble of excitement and conversation. She spied her parents dancing happily near the center of the crowd. Next to them, Louisa and Patrick were also smiling contentedly in each other's arms. She scanned the room further and found May and Samuel seated, as she would have guessed, comfortably on a settee that her mother had specifically ordered to be placed adjacent to the laid parquet dance floor so that May could enjoy the sights of the evening even though she couldn't dance. She saw Devon seated in the chair beside her brother. But she didn't see Adele.

She'd need to move to another angle, so she crawled to the window adjacent to where she'd been and craned her neck around the large rose bush in front, catching her sleeve on a thorn in the process.

"Well, now my dress is certainly ruined," she said aloud. She'd have to come up with an excuse for the mess she'd made of it at another time. Now she needed to find her sister.

She didn't see her sitting anywhere else in the room and began to feel the anxious pounding again in her chest. She looked back to Samuel, May, and Devon and realized Devon was looking intently out into the crowd of dancers. She followed his gaze and spotted them—Adele in the arms of Gabriel Desoto. He was whirling her across the floor with an expertise well beyond the levels of their humble county.

He's done this before, she thought as she studied her sister to ensure she was okay, but she needn't have worried. Adele was playing her part perfectly. She flushed with excitement as Gabriel twirled her out and back into his arms. He bent his head close and whispered something, and Adele rewarded his comment with a flashing smile and answer Amelia could not make out. She monitored the situation for a few more minutes, but since Adele seemed to be holding her own, Amelia left her sister to their task and sneaked back into the house in the direction opposite the one she'd come and up the steps to her room.

Safely away from judging eyes, she wearily undressed herself and shrugged into her nightgown. Then she chose a book on the shelf that she'd read at least a dozen times in recent years and lay down on her bed to find a way to pass the time. Her heart wasn't in it, however, even though she knew and loved every word. Within minutes she'd given up and decided to crochet instead. At least then she could use up some of her nervous energy. She went to her bureau and pulled open a drawer, selecting a soft yarn, winter white in color, and sat in her chair to begin. She'd finished almost an entire hand muff for the following Christmas before her door opened, and Adele entered swiftly, locking the door behind her.

"Well?" Amelia asked impatiently.

"For Heaven's sake, Millie, give me a minute to catch my breath after climbing those stairs in this dress! It has to weigh at least a hundred pounds," Adele complained as she turned around so that Amelia could help her escape the costume and corset.

"Talk while we get you out of this then," Amelia urged.

"Okay," she said, and whipped around. "I believe it worked!"

Amelia looked relieved. "I'm so glad! You were brilliant."

"Why do you say that?"

"I couldn't help myself and sneaked down to the garden to take a peek."

Adele was horrified. "Mercy, Amelia! You didn't! What would you have done if you'd been spotted?"

"I don't know. I'm sure I would have thought of something. A missing diamond broach or some such nonsense. Just please, go on!"

Adele sat down on the bed and patted the spot next to her. Amelia joined her and listened intently as Adele relayed the events of the evening. Gabriel had taken the bait when Devon introduced him to Adele. He was instantly smitten. And Devon hadn't even needed to pretend to be vying for her attention as Gabriel had apparently behaved like a perfect gentleman.

"That has to be the first decent thing I've ever heard about the man," Amelia grumbled, still bitter over her interaction with him earlier, which she then described to Adele.

"Oh how awful for you! Thank goodness Devon saw what was happening."

"Indeed," Amelia nodded.

Standing to leave, Adele suddenly turned and added, "I almost forgot to tell you about the dinner party!"

"What dinner party?"

"Aunt Louisa invited us all over for a party in two weeks to celebrate Uncle Patrick's birthday."

"Oh, that sounds lovely," Amelia smiled, slightly disappointed it had nothing to do with her plan. She was about to utter a generic goodnight when Adele concluded, "I invited Gabriel to attend as my escort."

Chapter 7

     .

The rain beat steadily on the window panes, creating a stream effect that made Amelia feel as if she were swimming instead of sitting cozily next to May in Louisa's parlor as they waited for dinner to be announced. Dusk had begun to settle outside, which made the storm seem even more ominous, as she found herself staring out into the darkness, wishing to be anywhere but where she was. She had overestimated her readiness for regular social visits. Without Ethan, she felt lost. They'd been together in one way or another for so long, she was used to having him there to turn to mid-conversation for his opinion on whatever topic led the day. Now she turned and there was no one there. She hadn't realized how dependent she'd been on him until those moments that came more often than she cared to admit. She thought someday she might feel differently, but right now she still felt as if a piece of herself was inexplicably gone.

The ride to the dinner at O'Brien's Plantation had been uneventful. Gabriel had arrived precisely on time, escorted Adele into the carriage, and had, since then, been very attentive, but not overly so. *He certainly knows how to behave as a gentleman,* Amelia mused, *even if he isn't one.* He had made sure to give Adele her space throughout the evening so far, yet he had been the first to assist her when she dropped her handkerchief. For her part, Adele behaved perfectly. She maintained a façade of a flattered and flirtatious schoolgirl as they'd been greeted by Aunt Louisa and continued as such now. Amelia was admittedly nervous. If Gabriel continued to behave so eloquently in public company, and there was no reason for her to spend time with him privately, she feared it might all be for naught. Up until this moment, he had shown no signs of slipping into the ugly, intimidating brute she'd encountered at the ball.

Someone patted her hand. "Millie," May whispered, shifting uncomfortably in her seat under the weight of the baby who could come any day now. "Your mother asked you a question."

Startled, Amelia turned her face back to the room. "Excuse me, Mother, I'm afraid I didn't hear you."

Juliette looked at her sternly, clearly bothered by her daughter's rudeness, and then said, "I was just telling Louisa that you and Devon had come close to wrapping up Ethan's affairs at the Bennigan offices, and we wanted to know if you thought Devon may be thinking of staying on here in Oak County permanently."

Devon had returned to the coast to wrap up a former case the previous week and was expected to return to Moon Springs on the weekend coach in a few days. Amelia quickly refocused her thoughts and frowned, "I'm really not quite sure. He doesn't seem to know exactly what he wants to do at this point. I think he enjoys Moon Springs, but it might not be enough to keep him here. He's quite successful in his practice, from what I hear. There's talk of his becoming a senior partner in the fall."

Louisa nodded enthusiastically. "Fabulous! Besides, he's a city boy. The city has so much more to offer than we do here. Can you imagine being able to attend the theater and symphony every night if you wanted? Gowns for every day of the week instead of having two ratty ones to choose from over and over again. It sounds delightful, and I can't possibly imagine anyone choosing this"—she gestured around the room —"over a setting like that."

Juliette smiled thoughtfully. "Well, now, I'm not sure, Louisa. I was raised in Paris, and I much prefer the quietness of the country to the constant bustle of the city. It's a marvelous mix of both worlds here. We have the occasional enjoyment of fineries, yet it's not a daunting task to survive each social season. "Besides," she added, "you could always order more dresses from Savannah or Atlanta. Or I could even give you the name of my seamstress back home in France. I'm sure she'd do wonders with your figure and coloring, and all you'd need to do is send her your measurements and color preferences."

"Well, that would be the day," Louisa huffed. "Patrick would wring my neck if I ordered another gown when I have no real place to wear it, wouldn't you Patrick?"

Patrick chuckled. "That depends, dear, on if owning another frivolous frock like the ones you like would be a good return on investment. Could you demand that the delivery be accompanied by a textile factory owner who would come and see our crops for the year and buy it all up to make copies of your dress to sell in all the local shops? If the answer is yes, then by all means, order away."

Michael laughed loudly at Patrick's typically practical response. "Well, dear sister, he sure put that issue to rest, didn't he? I wish I were that clever, Patrick. It might have saved me thousands of dollars over the past twenty years or so."

Louisa huffed, disgusted at the mockery her husband and brother had made of her sincere interest in all things fashionable and high class. "It's always about the money with you men, isn't it? What good is it to make all the money in the world if you won't spend a penny?"

"That's all well and good until you've stopped making any money at all, and you still continue to spend," Patrick retorted, uncharacteristically short in tone.

"And that's when you use good common sense and find a different way to make money. If you would only just consider joining Michael at the Mercantile, this would not even be a discussion," Louisa argued.

"Or, if the mercantile business isn't for you, I'd be happy to discuss the plans I have for this budding county," Gabriel interjected. These were the first interesting words he'd spoken all afternoon to anyone but Adele, and everyone turned to look at him in surprise as if they'd almost forgotten he was there.

He continued with eagerness, his audience suddenly attentive. "The railways are coming here, there's no doubt about it, and now is the time to jump in —when the industry is in the early stages. That's where the real money is."

Patrick was clearly intrigued. "Yes," he said slowly, "Ethan had mentioned something along those lines to me before he—" he stopped prematurely, unconsciously turning his head towards Amelia.

She smiled slightly, "Please, Uncle Patrick. It's fine. Don't stop on my account."

Louisa stood up abruptly. "No more talk about any of this, please, gentleman. This is my dinner party, and I won't hear of it. Mr. Desoto, thank you, but we're not interested in the railroad business. We've got plenty to deal with here at the plantation, and any extra time will be spent learning the mercantile business, something I think Patrick would be marvelous at." She smiled sweetly, but her tone betrayed her annoyance.

Amelia hadn't specifically told her aunt about Ethan's deal with Desoto, but she was a smart woman and had surely deduced as much. She was sure Louisa had no interest in getting her money caught up alongside the Bennigans'.

Crossing the room to stand next to Louisa, Amelia grabbed her hand and said, "I agree. This discussion is completely monotonous. Come and show me the new set of curtains you ordered for the library! I've heard they're stunning."

Louisa's face brightened to its usual gaiety, and she bustled from the room, gesturing for Amelia to follow her. Adele also rose and excused herself to go look as well. Amelia slowed to wait for her in the hallway.

"I can't believe Gabriel had the nerve to bring up his business in front of our family!" Adele whispered to Amelia as they walked in the direction of the library.

"I know. He's either very desperate or very stupid if he doesn't realize that no one else associated with our family will be handing him a dime. It is good for our plan, though, that he feels so safe to freely discuss it. That must mean he doesn't suspect that we're trying to expose him as Ethan's killer, or he would be playing closer to his chest."

Louisa poked her head back into the hallway. "Are you coming girls?"

"Yes, ma'am." Adele smiled, and they quickly entered the room. Louisa described, in detail, the great lengths she had gone to secure the exclusive fabric from New York. After months of waiting, it had finally arrived the week prior. The sisters were admiring the softness and subtle sheen as the butler came and announced that dinner was to be served in the dining room presently.

Everyone gathered in Louisa's dining room. She stood at the foot of the table and raised her glass. "To my Patrick. Happy birthday, my love!"

Patrick nodded his thanks, and they all took a sip of the bubbling champagne. Amelia relished the bubbles tickling their way down her throat as she looked around at her family. Everyone seemed happy and smiling. Even May. For the first moment in over a month, Amelia felt a bit of serenity again, and she was so grateful that things were starting slowly to take on a semblance of normalcy. She had realized during the weeks since the ball that her mother had been partially right. Ethan would not have wanted her to live the rest of her life in infinite sadness. He would want her to celebrate at times like this. He had loved life, and she pledged to try to do the same. She sneaked a glance at Adele while everyone congratulated Patrick on reaching the ripe old age of sixty. On the outside, her sister was beaming under the attentions of Gabriel. But Amelia could sense an anxious sadness behind her happy eyes, and she knew she, too, would not be able to fully move on until Desoto rotted in jail for what he'd done to Ethan. She only hoped her sister wouldn't have to suffer his company much longer before she was able to prove it.

After a savory dinner of broiled pheasant and pecan stuffing, they all withdrew into the small drawing room that also served as the daytime parlor. Louisa suggested a game of bridge. Juliette, Samuel, and May gladly obliged, and they settled at a small table in the corner of the room. Michael and Patrick were enjoying a drink of brandy by the fireplace. That left Adele, Amelia, and Gabriel in the chairs in the middle of the room. She could see Gabriel was anxious for her to leave them alone so he might engage Adele in a more intimate conversation, which made Amelia's skin crawl. But she caught Adele's eye, and her sister gave her an encouraging nod. They wouldn't get anywhere unless Adele got to know Gabriel more intimately. Taking her sister's cue, Amelia stood and excused herself to use the powder room.

She knew Adele needed some time to pry more information out of Gabriel, so she wandered slowly up and down the hall, mindlessly studying the family paintings. She looked at the portrait of her cousins,

Henry and Harry, when they were teenagers. Both boys looked so much like Louisa. She missed them both tremendously, but both were leading successful lives as partners in a farming supply company up in Virginia, so she rarely saw them. Amelia couldn't imagine how lonely her life would be if her siblings weren't around.

Her back was to the drawing room door when she heard the panel slide open. She turned around and was alarmed to see Gabriel exiting.

"I'm surprised to see you away from Adele, Mr. Desoto. I can't imagine she was happy to see you leave." She tried to encourage him but wondered anxiously if he was seeing right through her false enthusiasm. He made her so nervous. She felt every inch of her body start to tremble as he approached her slowly. She gripped her skirt with her hands, trying to steady them.

"Louisa called her over for advice on her bridge hand, so I took the opportunity to seek you out."

"I can't imagine why. I'm afraid I'm rotten company these days."

He came closer, but stopped a few feet short of arms reach, thankfully. "I find that I must apologize to you, Miss Sullivan, for my behavior at the ball. I was incredibly rude. I should never have intimated that you were responsible for repaying Ethan's debt. I apologize for any discomfort you may have felt as a result of our conversation."

Her jaw dropped, but she recovered quickly. "I'm not quite sure I understand, Mr. Desoto."

He shrugged his shoulders. "At the time I was solely concerned about my money. But since then, I've had the pleasure of getting to know your family and realize that you're nothing short of the most honorable of people, and thus, pose no threat to me or my business. And I can see that if anyone could have repaid Ethan's debt more quickly to me, he or she would have. He seems to have been the most ambitious of your lot. I don't think the railroad business would be tame enough for anyone else around here, judging from the reaction I received today," he chuckled, "so I'm assuming if you could get me out of your hair by giving me what I came for, you would have done it by now."

"So, you're still waiting for your money," Amelia crossed her arms, challenging him.

"Yes. But I realize now that your family won't be able to help me get it. Now May and Devon, on the other hand." His eyes drifted back to the parlor door.

"I'll stop you right there, Mr. Desoto." She said his name with indignant emphasis. "You will leave May out of this. She has no more access to Ethan or Bennett's money than I have. She gave up her financial ties to her family when she married my brother. And if you haven't eyes in your head, she's expecting a baby soon. So you'll cause her any discomfort over my dead body."

As she said them, she couldn't believe the words had come out of her mouth and sounded so sincere to boot.

Gabriel stepped back as he raised his hands in defeat, clearly amused by her boldness. "Fine. Your sister-in-law is off limits. But I'm not going away, as I said before. I've just decided that using you is not the way to do it."

He turned and took a few steps back toward the door but continued talking.

"I can't promise to leave Devon alone, though, because, as I see it, he is the only one able to help me regain my money. So you'll have to resign your pretty little self to that."

Her blood boiled at his patronizing tone, and she put her hands on her hips. "Your compliments mean nothing to me, Mr. Desoto. You may have my sister fooled, but I see right through your charm. I wouldn't be surprised if you killed Ethan yourself because he just looked at you wrong."

Her hand flew to her mouth when she realized the weight of what she'd just said. She braced herself for his response but was surprised by what she saw in his eyes when he turned around to stare at her in bewilderment. The darkness was gone, and genuine shock had taken its place.

He was silent for a moment as if considering her words, then burst into a maniacal laughter that resonated down the long hallway. "Me? You think I killed Ethan?"

He stepped back towards her, and she backed up instinctively until her shoulders were against the wall.

"What, may I ask, would I gain by doing that? Have you not heard everything I've been saying these past weeks? Ethan's death was essentially the worst thing that happened to my business in this county. I paid off all of his debts. So I have no capital left. And as you can see, I'm having a challenging time recovering my losses. No, Ethan's murder was most inconvenient for me, Miss Sullivan. It's delayed my business plans in other areas of the state by at least six months while I stay here trying to clean up his mess. I, of all people, had the biggest reason to want him alive."

"You?" she argued. "You think you had a better reason to want him alive than me? His fiancée? I think not. And your pitiful story about losing your money does nothing for my heart strings, Mr. Desoto. Based solely upon the evidence of our two infuriating encounters, you're a brute of a man who probably wouldn't bat an eye at having someone killed if they angered you enough. Perhaps Ethan told you he couldn't repay you."

"Well, thankfully we don't have to worry about that, Miss Sullivan, because that's not what happened."

"You'll forgive me if I don't believe you," she replied. "You seem to do a good job convincing people you're such a gentleman when clearly you're not. I don't believe a word you say."

He frowned and shook his head. "That's your loss, then, I'm afraid. But I do hope you'll keep your foolish suspicions to yourself. You wouldn't want to anger the wrong person."

She watched as he walked back into the room, plastering his charming smile back on his face just in time. She walked to the stairs and sat, putting her head in her hands. She'd ruined everything. She just couldn't hold her temper. It always got the better of her. Her father would say that was the Irish in her, but whatever it was, she was angry with herself. How was she going to get Adele out of this now that Gabriel knew she suspected him of murder? He was a smart man, so he would know that she wouldn't willingly let her sister spend time with him if she thought that way. She sighed, standing back up, realizing she'd been gone a long time.

The rest of the afternoon passed without further incident and, mercifully, without the need for Amelia to converse with Desoto directly. When they were finally home that evening, she recounted the discussion she'd had in the hallway with Gabriel to her sister. Adele was concerned, but undeterred, much to Amelia's surprise.

"Adele," she carried a serious overtone in her voice. "I'm just not sure it's worth the risk at this point. Honestly, he terrifies me."

Adele considered this for a moment. "Well, he's certainly arrogant. I'm just not sure he's capable of murder, Millie. He seems to be genuinely put out over Ethan's death. From what I gather his business is indefinitely paralyzed until he can regain what he lost in the railroads. Maybe he really didn't do it."

Amelia refused to believe what she was hearing. "Oh, please. Don't tell me he's fooled you, too, Adele. He practically threatened my life today when he suspected I might mention theory to the sheriff. It was him. I'm sure of it. He's evil, he's well-connected, and he's angry. That's all the evidence I need."

Some days later, Adele rushed into the library where Amelia was enjoying a warm cup of tea and her favorite novel. Amelia looked up, alarmed at the flush on Adele's cheeks as she picked up the book off her lap and sat down beside her on the settee.

Adele could barely contain herself. "Millie, I think I've discovered something that may be of help!"

Amelia sat up straighter enlivened a new sense of urgency. "What is it?"

"Well, Gabriel asked if I would enjoy a walk into town today, and at first I really couldn't stand the thought of spending any more time with him, but something inside me made me say yes, and how glad am I that I did!"

Trying not to seem impatient, Amelia nodded to encourage her sister to continue. "Well, he wanted to take me to lunch at the inn, but his carriage was being repaired, so we walked along the main roads into town since, of course, I didn't want to show him any of the back ways. The walk itself was pleasant enough but hardly exciting. Lunch was tolerable. You know how much I love Mrs. Handley's chicken soup. But I hardly learned anything new that might be important about him. He told me about growing up in a city, how it differed from the country, and all such nonsense. I was beginning to feel like the whole thing was for naught when he suggested we walk along the river to return home. Well, we were only a few minutes outside of town when we came upon a stranger going the opposite direction."

"What did he look like? Did he say his name? Have you ever seen him around here before?" Amelia fired questions in rapid succession.

Adele was annoyed. "Amelia. I said he was a *stranger.* And no, he didn't say his name, but he certainly knew Gabriel, and Gabriel knew him—it's just he didn't want me to know it. He tried to walk past with just an impassive nod, but the man stopped him. If I wasn't so nervous, I would have laughed because the man was clearly confused as to why Mr. Desoto was pretending they'd never met."

"It's not surprising. He probably has all sorts of sordid acquaintances he'd rather not own up to."

"That's exactly what I thought!" Adele agreed. "Anyway, the man tried to start discussing something with Gabriel about a contract in Savannah and how things were not progressing as smoothly as he'd hoped, and what should he do about it. Well, at that moment, I would have given anything for you to see Gabriel's face, Millie. He was furious! He turned dark red, and his fists balled up. He said, 'How dare you bring up such unsettling matters as business in front of a lady.' At first I was frightened he was going to strike the man in front of me because he marched right up to him and put his nose an inch away from the other man's. But instead he just whispered something in his ear, and then the man scurried on his way. I wasn't going to let him get away without explaining to me, so I put on my best innocent girl face and asked, 'Mr. Desoto, what was the matter with that poor man?' He must have realized he still looked angry because he finally smiled and tried to brush me off by saying, 'Nothing, Miss Sullivan. I'm sure there's just a mix-up in some paperwork that he will work out.' But I kept asking questions. I said, 'Why did you not stop to talk to him at first?' And, I sadly admit, I thought I had him there, but he wormed his way out of it. He said, 'Miss Sullivan, I was simply enjoying our conversation so much I didn't realize I knew him when he first passed.' I couldn't figure out anything else to say after that, so I just had to pretend I was satisfied, but if you ask me, Millie, I think that there was something to do with that contract the man was referring to that Gabriel didn't want me to hear. Father talks about business in front of us all the time. So, it can't just be because I'm a girl. It must be something he really didn't want me to know!"

Amelia listened to the whole story with interest and then sat back to think. She ventured, "Well, it could be the contract itself, or, even more likely, it is who he signed the contract with he doesn't want to reveal. I suspect it's with someone any decent person would find objectionable, or he wouldn't have gone to such great lengths to avoid discussing anything with the man."

Either way, it was indeed extremely helpful. She turned back to her sister and gave her a hug. "Thank you, Adele. You're right. That's exactly the type of thing we need to look into. Hopefully, Devon and I can ask some questions around town and in Savannah to see if we can figure out who Desoto may be working with and if his alliances could be connected with Ethan's death."

Having completed her account of the afternoon, Adele reclined back in a relaxed pose. "Now if we could just meet another stranger on the road who could throw evidence in our lap proving Bennett is innocent." Adele crossed her arms and sat back, taking her own sip of Amelia's tea.

Placing her hand lovingly over her sister's, Amelia smiled. "We will, Adele. Don't worry. It will all be okay."

She stood up and went to her father's desk to borrow some paper and a pen. She jotted down a quick note for Devon, asking him to come the next day so she could update him on what Adele had learned. She needed his help now more than ever. Brave as she was, she wasn't about to start investigating a threat like Gabriel Desoto alone.

Devon arrived promptly the next morning, and Amelia suggested they take a walk to avoid unwanted eavesdropping by the servants or her parents. Thankfully, Juliette didn't balk at the suggestion this time, so the two were able to leave alone without any fuss.

It was an exceptionally warm spring day, so they decided to walk through the path in the woods to the river road. As they approached the creek bed where Ethan had died, Amelia hesitated for a moment. Sensing her apprehension, Devon extended his hand.

"Here, take my hand. We'll go past together," he said. "This place makes me uneasy as well, almost as if it's haunted. Although that makes me sound like a meek ninny, doesn't it?"

"I don't think that's silly at all. A horrible thing happened here. And it happened so recently still, it does almost seem haunted in a way," she agreed. "I certainly don't like going down here, but it's the only way to get to the river quickly, and I absolutely won't stop going there. I suppose I'll have to get used to it. I'm just glad I'm not the only one who feels so uneasy," she assured him, patting his arm.

They briskly walked in silence, eyes fixed straight ahead and past the scene of Ethan's murder;

both breathing an audible sigh of relief when they were at last beyond it.

"Well, that wasn't so bad," Devon said, unconvincingly.

"What do you mean? It was horrible!" Amelia retorted. "But we can't avoid it forever, so we might as well get used to it."

"I hope you're right."

They emerged out of the forest path onto the road that ran adjacent to the river and crossed to the edge closest to the water. The scent of the calm waters flowing gently towards town immediately soothed Amelia's uneasiness, and she was finally able to broach the subject she'd summoned him for in the first place. She did her best to relay the details of Adele's outing with Gabriel the day before correctly. Then she offered her own interpretation of what had happened. Devon was silent for a moment, deep in thought, but then he concurred.

"It is absolutely suspicious. From what you're telling me, he most definitely tried to avoid having to converse with the fellow in front of your sister. And I agree with her assessment that it wasn't simply because it was business-related, or he would have at least acknowledged the man."

"Precisely," said Amelia.

She was about to continue when Devon's eyes darted up and he hollered. She turned to look behind her, but something yanked her arm, and she tumbled head first over the edge of the river bank. As she rolled end over end, skidding along the grass, she caught a glimpse of a horse gallop by on the road. She tried to catch herself on the steep grassy bank, but the hill was still slippery from the hard rain that had fallen days before, so she helplessly watched the water get closer and closer until, at last, she slid into the freezing current. Thankfully, the water was not deep, and she was able to push up onto her knees and then stood unassisted. She turned to look at Devon who had managed to grab a root of a tree on the way down and hadn't gone into the water.

"Millie, are you all right?" he shouted.

"I'm standing aren't I? Yes, of course, I'm fine," she assured him, grabbing his outstretched hand. He pulled her up out of the water, and they managed to climb back up to the road. Once on solid ground, they both sat down, hearts racing and clothes muddy.

"What happened?" Amelia was so confused as to why the rider of the horse hadn't steered away from them.

"That idiot rode his horse right towards you. I've never seen a rider on a footpath like this going so fast." Devon shook his head. "I know he saw us because when I shouted at him he looked right at me."

"I don't understand."

"Neither do I," he said. "He must have had some sort of emergency in town and was just looking right through us."

"But you would think when you'd shouted you would have snapped him out of his reverie."

"You would think, but even when he made eye contact, it was almost as if he was looking through me instead of at me."

Amelia bent down to examine her torn and muddy dress. "I'd have a much easier time forgiving him for this mess if I knew he'd had a true emergency and wasn't in his right mind. But," she said as she climbed back up onto the road from the embankment, "seeing as we're both okay, I suppose we should head back to the house and get cleaned up. We won't wash this mud off sitting here angry at a stranger."

Devon followed suit, but Amelia could tell by his stoic face that he didn't believe their close encounter had been the result of a careless rider. She wanted to ignore the implications, but it was clear. He thought that man had run them off the road on purpose.

Chapter 8

Amelia's fingers caressed the ebony sheen of the horse's muscular neck gently as she placed an affectionate kiss on the top of his leathery muzzle, and he grunted a low nicker in return, grateful for the attention she showed him in comparison to the usual gruff indifference he received from Gabriel Desoto. The Sullivans had been invited to the manor where Gabriel had taken up residence when he'd realized he would be in Oak County longer than he'd originally intended. He'd ordered his impressive team of fox hunting horses shipped in from Savannah to entertain himself and was all too happy to show off his possessions.

For once not needing to feign interest in something related to Desoto, Amelia inquired as to the beautiful creature's name.

"That's Ebony Road," Gabriel smiled greedily. "He's won me purses worth thousands of dollars in fox hunting."

"He's beautiful," she remarked, brushing Ebony's mane. "And so sweet."

"A horse's temperament means nothing to me as long as he does what he was bred to do," Desoto retorted gruffly as he walked ahead in the stable to join Adele.

Amelia turned back to Ebony and put her hands on both sides of the stallion's face and planted a final kiss. "Don't you listen to that horrible man," she whispered. "You're precious, and I think that is much more important than how much money you bring in to line his seedy pockets."

She gave his neck one more pat as Louisa and Patrick entered the barn door nearest her.

"Aunt Louisa. Uncle Patrick. I'm so glad you could join us!"

Louisa greeted Amelia with her usual level of intimacy, but she noticed that Patrick was not his normal, jovial self.

Amelia stepped back from her aunt to eye her uncle. "Uncle Patrick, you look positively ghastly. Whatever is the matter?"

Patrick shook his head in frustration and moved past the women, grumbling to himself as he trudged away to catch up to Michael and Juliette.

Amelia looked to Louisa for an explanation, but she just shrugged her shoulders. "I'm sure I don't know what's wrong with him, really. He mentioned something about the farmers' union legislation being turned down from the docket in Atlanta, but all that talk is a foreign language to me. So, I just pat his hand, kiss his cheek and tell him it will all be all right. That's the best a wife can expect to do in times like these."

Frowning, Amelia linked arms with her aunt and began to trudge through the straw and dirt on the barn floor, ignoring the hem of her dress that was dragging stubbornly each step she took. She couldn't imagine having an approach to marital strife like that of her aunt. Had Ethan lived, she was sure after time they would have been of a simpatico understanding of their financial situation, even if he hadn't intended to allow her any initial input. But Louisa and her mother came from a different era. They would likely never see things the same way as she.

They stopped to admire several more horses on the way out of the rear barn door that led to the pasture where Gabriel had prepared a grand picnic for his guests. Amelia took a seat at the corner of the large blanket which had been spread on the ground, leaving room for May and the baby to spread out. The rest of the party gathered for lemonade under a big oak tree.

"Hello, everyone!" Samuel called as he drove his wagon up to join the rest of the family. He hopped down from the driver's seat and went around to the back to help May and the baby down from the bed. Devon exited via the other side and grabbed the baby's belongings that May had packed into a pretty white basket. He placed the basket down beside Amelia and greeted the party.

"That silly boy always looks so ridiculous driving that old wagon around. And now with a baby! I don't know how May can stand it!" Louisa whispered to Juliette, who smiled knowingly.

"Samuel is just a simple man who doesn't care to look elegant. He favors practicality, and the wagon clearly served that purpose on a nice day like today when they could all get a few extra minutes of sunshine and fresh air and not be trapped in a stuffy carriage cabin."

Juliette rose from her seat to greet May and take the baby from her so she could have a much needed break. "Sit down, May," she said. "I'll hold Ethan for a few minutes." She tickled the baby's cheek lovingly, and took him over to see his grandfather.

May collapsed down beside Amelia and sipped the lemonade Samuel handed her. "I tell you, Millie, he is the sweetest baby, but I just can't get him to sleep! It's like he's already itching to get outdoors and play every second of the day and night. And he's not yet three weeks old!"

Laughing, Amelia gazed at her fiancé's namesake, cooing in her mother's arms. She had been so touched when Samuel and May had named their son after Ethan, and apparently the child had the zest for life that her Ethan had possessed also. She adored him. He was a bright light amidst the dark year they'd had.

Devon sat down next to May on the blanket. "Have you told Millie the news?"

"No, I haven't," she said.

"Is it about Bennett?" Amelia asked excitedly. It had been two months, and now they couldn't even visit him as he'd been moved to the state penitentiary in Atlanta the week before when his trial date had been announced.

"Yes. I've filed the paperwork contesting his arrest and the lack of evidence and asked that the case be dismissed from the circuit courts."

"Oh, wonderful! Hopefully, the judge will be reasonable and realize that the state has no evidence against him."

Amelia glanced at Adele, who was attentively listening to Gabriel go on about his conquests in fox hunting. Her poor sister had been carrying on this charade for several weeks now, and Amelia could see that it was wearing her down. Her normally beautiful eyes were now dull and tired. Amelia could tell Adele was losing hope that they would ever gather enough evidence against Desoto to free Bennett. She had to admit that her determination was waning also. If Devon's petition wasn't successful, she was terrified that Bennett might actually be put on trial for Ethan's murder, and she really had no idea what the outcome of that would be. Not only could the sheriff's office produce its evidence, but who knew how far Gabriel's money could reach if he knew they really suspected him. She was sure he could have Bennett condemned if he wanted to.

Adele turned to look at her family and stood. "Who would like to join Mr. Desoto and me for a ride?" she asked, gesturing towards the barn. "It's such a beautiful day, and he tells me there's a lovely path that follows the outskirts of a meadow full of wildflowers! I'd love to see them!"

Amelia could sense the desperation in Adele's voice, and shuddering at the thought of subjecting her sister to any more time alone with Desoto, Amelia stood as well.

"That sounds refreshing! Devon, would you care to accompany us as well?"

"Absolutely!" He hopped up, trotting ahead to walk with Gabriel.

Amelia was glad he'd agreed to join them. She'd grown fond of having Devon around; he brought a sense of normalcy back to her life, and she could count on his being there, a steady, level-headed presence. Plus, he made her feel much safer whenever Gabriel Desoto was around. She knew he wouldn't dare try to harm or even threaten her if Devon was also present.

"Amelia, dear! Do wait for me!" Juliette caught up quickly, taking Amelia's arm to steady herself when her shoe slid in the dirt.

"I was wondering if you would join us, Mother."

"Oh, you know me! I never turn down a ride!" Juliette said, laughing. She had grown up with an estate stable of nearly one hundred horses. She was an expert in the saddle and had taught each of her own children the skill at a very early age.

They all entered the barn and were met by Desoto's stablehand, who brought out horses for each of them to ride. Adele was on an Appaloosa beauty named Snowcap, while Devon was given a red roan stallion simply called Sir.

As the stablehand led Ebony Road out of his stall, Gabriel pointed to Amelia. "Take him to that lovely young lady, Thomas. She's been eyeing Ebony since she arrived this morning."

While Amelia did so want to ride the gorgeous horse, she gestured to her mother. "No, please, Thomas, let my mother ride Ebony Road. He seems like such a gentle fellow, and he's shorter than the others; my mother is quite petite."

Gabriel looked surprised. "Why, Miss Sullivan, I'm shocked. From the way you bonded with him earlier, I'm surprised to still find him here in my stables and not back at Sullivan's Pine in yours! Are you certain you don't want to ride him? I'm sure we can find another equally tame horse for Mrs. Sullivan"—he nodded politely to Juliette—"not to imply that she can't handle any horse we'd give her. I can sense you are educated in the equestrian field, Mrs. Sullivan."

Juliette returned his smile courteously. "You're ever so kind, Mr. Desoto, but I think I will take Amelia's suggestion. My legs are quite short, and I do tend to have difficulty getting on and off if the horse is too large. Ebony Road seems like he is just right for me." Taking Thomas's hand to step onto the block, Juliette seamlessly mounted the horse and led him to join in line with the others.

Gabriel frowned at Amelia. "What a disappointment. I do feel as if you and Ebony Road would have made the perfect pair."

Agitated at his persistence on the subject, Amelia ignored his last comment and gratefully accepted the new horse Thomas brought from the furthest stall. This dapple horse, aptly named Pebbles, was a tall, austere mare that behaved properly and followed the others in an orderly fashion, although she certainly lacked the free spirit Amelia had sensed in Ebony Road, but it didn't matter.

The manor Gabriel had leased for six months lay north of Moon Springs by several miles. Amelia had never been in that area. It was beautifully ensconced by lush forest, and the foothills of the Appalachian Mountains were ever so slightly closer here than at home. Far from the flats of the river basin, the land sloped gently, offering the most beautiful vistas as they made their way towards the meadow Gabriel had promised Adele.

"How long does it take to get to the meadow, Mr. Desoto?" Adele asked nervously as the horses followed single file along a slender part of the path.

"Oh, it's not much further," he replied. "Perhaps another mile or so."

They were now along a slight ridge overlooking a stone quarry on the bordering property. The view was brilliant, but the narrowness of the rocky path made Amelia slightly squeamish. Normally she felt completely at ease on a horse, but she could sense that even-keeled Pebbles was also slightly unnerved by the trickiness of the path, and she reached down to pat her neck. "There, there, girl. We'll be all right. Just a bit longer on this part." Her vain attempts at comforting the horse didn't help as Pebbles hoof caught on a sharp boulder, and she skidded forward slightly. Although it was just a slight misstep, it was enough to cause a chain reaction behind them as the other horses spooked in response to the commotion.

"Whoa!" Devon hollered, trying to calm Sir who tripped back slightly before steadying himself.

Amelia turned, gesturing to Devon that he should try to go ahead of her to allow Pebbles room at the back when she heard a shriek directly in front of her. She craned her neck around to see her mother, legs dangling, desperately clinging to the mane of a furious Ebony Road. The horse let out a horrendous whinny and reared again. He finally set all four feet back on the path but stomped and snorted ferociously. Something was terribly wrong.

Had there been room enough for two horses to stand side by side on the path Amelia could have

134

simply ridden alongside her mother and helped her over onto Pebbles until they could calm Ebony down, but they were still on the ledge, and it was definitely not wide enough.

Amelia tried to assess what had spooked the horse so severely when he suddenly reared again, this time nearly throwing Juliette off his back and over the edge of the cliff.

"Mother!" Amelia screamed.

Juliette yanked his head back towards his shoulder to draw his attention and prevent him from bolting, but it was useless. Ebony Road furiously tore ahead, nearly running the horses ahead off the widening path as he stormed by. Amelia waited in horror for another horse to lose its footing and was relieved when they all stayed put while the crazed animal ran by them.

Gabriel, who was at the front of the line, tried to reach out and grab the reins as Ebony ran past him, but he wasn't able to get a good grip, and the horse easily slipped by.

Thinking perhaps the horse had just been momentarily startled by Pebbles, Amelia was alarmed when Ebony continued sprinting even when he was back again on the normal path. She could see Juliette clinging to the reins, dangerously close to sliding off the rear as he hurdled ahead towards the meadow that was now in sight. If she fell off at this speed, her mother could easily die.

"Devon! We have to catch her!" Amelia yelled. She dug her heels into Pebbles and jumpstarted the mare on a fast gallop after Ebony, Devon following. Sir was much faster, and Amelia was relieved to see he was recovering the distance between the two of them and Juliette quickly.

As she raced towards her mother, who was now shouting at Ebony in desperation to stop, Amelia tried to think. What had happened to Ebony? Something had either spooked him out of his wits, or he was in pain and trying to escape it. If it was his legs, he would be limping, not sprinting. It must be something else. Something he was trying to escape from. What had changed on that ledge?

"The reins!" Amelia screamed, praying Devon would hear her. "Devon, tell her to drop the reins! They're hurting him!"

She screamed the same thing over and over as she urged Pebbles to catch them. Finally, she saw Devon had closed the distance between himself and Juliette and was now riding in pace alongside her. Devon leaned over and shouted to her, and Amelia saw her mother shake her head. If she let go of her weakening grip on the reins she would slide off because Ebony's mane was now out of reach.

She took a deep breath and screamed at the top of her lungs. "Mother! Do as he says! Drop the reins!"

She saw Juliette's head tilt as she recognized her daughter's cries. She turned a petrified face to Devon and closed her eyes, simultaneously letting go of the reins and leaning forward to grab hold of the horse's mane.

The relief on the horse's part was instantaneous. He immediately slowed to a trot, and Devon quickly hauled Juliette onto his horse. Ebony trotted another few feet, then stopped altogether.

Amelia caught up quickly and jumped off her horse, running breathlessly to her mother. Juliette dismounted Sir and threw her arms around Amelia, tears streaming down her cheeks.

"Oh, Millie! I didn't know what to do! Thank you!" She turned to Devon, who had climbed down as well, and grabbed his hand. "Thank you, Devon. You saved my life."

Amelia's attention shifted to the horse. She had to remove whatever had caused him such anguish. She calmly spoke his name and took a step in Ebony's direction as the rest of the riders caught up.

"I'm glad you're okay, Mrs. Sullivan. Amelia! Stay back from him. He's mad!" Devon warned.

His stern warning didn't deter Amelia as she slowly approached Ebony Road. She had to figure out what had happened to that poor horse. He hadn't just lost his mind. Something had hurt him badly and caused him to run like that. She said his name gently as she approached, softly rubbing his back and neck as she walked around to his face. As she came closer, she could see a trickle of blood coming out of his mouth.

"Oh, sweet boy, what happened to you?" she reached out to get a closer look.

He jerked his head back, but she calmly rubbed his nose and repeated her soothing words, and he eventually relaxed his neck and allowed her to unstrap the bit from his mouth. Gently, she pulled the bit out, and her suspicions were confirmed.

Gabriel and Adele had joined the group, and Gabriel swung down off his horse, stomping up to

Ebony Road with his whip drawn, but Amelia stepped in between them.

"Don't you dare!" she yelled.

"Are you out of your mind? He nearly killed your mother, the beast!" Gabriel tried to push her aside and raised his arm to strike the horse, but Amelia grabbed his elbow.

"It wasn't his fault!" she insisted. "Look!"

"What?" he growled.

"There were barbs in his bit! They ripped his mouth open. He was hurting and scared and when Mother pulled on the reins it hurt worse, so he didn't know what to do!"

She shoved the barb-clad bit up to his face. He looked down, his face registering vague confusion, but she didn't believe it for one second.

"Mr. Desoto, it's obvious that you were trying to kill me!"

"Excuse me?" He stepped back, his face contorted into a snarl.

"No wonder you were so disappointed when I wasn't going to ride Ebony. You knew I liked him, and you put barbs in his bit so that if I had to pull back on the reins at any point he'd go crazy and take off. You knew this was going to happen! You just didn't count on me insisting my mother ride him instead."

"You've lost your mind!" Gabriel shouted, stepping back farther. "I have no idea how that happened to him!"

"Yes, you do! You did it yourself. Or had Thomas do it. How else do you explain what happened? He certainly didn't have barbs in his mouth when I met him earlier. Someone put them there. You're the only one with a reason to!" Amelia cried.

"And what reason is that?" he demanded.

"Either kill me or scare me into helping you get your money, of course!" she answered, angrier than ever. She didn't even care if he knew her suspicions now. It was over. Her mother had nearly died because of her. Her plan to expose him had failed. He was too dangerous.

"Amelia!" Adele said.

"We're going back to the stable, Adele, and we're leaving." Amelia turned to Desoto. "You'll be lucky if my father doesn't have you arrested for attempted murder. But I can tell you if you ever come near anyone in my family again, I will ensure he does."

Amelia got back on her horse and galloped as fast as the mare would go back to the stables. Adele and Devon's horses followed. Gabriel didn't try to follow, apparently deciding to walk back with Ebony Road. Amelia didn't care. He was a murderer, and now she knew it. Adele had been right. He was too dangerous to try to expose on her own. She'd nearly lost her mother because of her naïve stupidity. She'd have to find another way to clear Bennett. She wouldn't let Gabriel even lay eyes on another member of her family again.

Chapter 9

     Gray skies, appropriately glum and foreboding, accompanied Amelia and Devon as they ascended the imposing brick steps into the county courthouse in Smithton on the morning of Bennett's trial. The ancient building rose from the city square in a menacing fashion, threatening to squash out all hopes for those hoping to defend themselves. Amelia's chest pounded as Devon tugged on the heavy door that opened into the courtroom.

     She immediately saw the back of Bennett's head, his hair long, combed back and oiled. He wore a newly pressed navy wool suit that May had sent ahead for the proceedings. Although the material was nice and clean and likely the best suit she could find, wool was extremely hot for the summer, and Bennett was already sweating profusely.

     Amelia encouragingly patted his shoulder as she slid onto the bench directly behind the defense table. Devon joined Bennett up front and opened his satchel to remove a stack of papers inches high.

     "Try to relax," she heard Devon say. "Once they see how little evidence the county has against you, they'll dismiss the case. Just stay calm and sincere."

     Bennett nodded somberly and turned to give Amelia a half-smile.

     "Thank you for coming, Millie."

     Amelia frowned. "Of course I came. I simply can't believe it's come to this. I've tried so hard to convince the sheriff to drop the charges. He just won't…."

Bennett held up a hand. "It's all right, Amelia. I have faith in Devon, here, to straighten this all out."

As Devon and Bennett began to discuss specific strategy, Amelia attempted to engage her nerves by familiarizing herself with the room. It was a relatively large courtroom compared to the ones she had previously seen. The musty smell of old, rotting wood prevailed against the half-hearted attempt at disguise by pink day lilies which had been placed on small tables in the corner.

She looked towards the witness bench where Sheriff Hastings and Nancy, the maid, sat quietly. Nancy was visibly nervous, silently wringing her handkerchief between her hands. Amelia only hoped she was able to withstand the pressure from the prosecutors without too much emotional trauma.

There were few other spectators aside from the witnesses—just a man with a pinstripe suit and notebook that Amelia assumed was a journalist and a few other men dressed less professionally. One of the men looked familiar, but she couldn't quite place him.

The door opposite the main entrance slowly swung open as the judge entered the courtroom from his chambers.

"All rise," the bailiff called.

Devon and Bennett obediently stood, and Amelia did the same, nodding her head at the judge even though she knew he wasn't looking at her. Suddenly the fact that they were attending Ethan's murder trial, and Bennett was the accused, hit her, and she felt dizzy. Her heart ached for Bennett and the situation she had helped put him in.

Please let this end here, she prayed.

After the introductory remarks from the judge describing how the events of the day would transpire, he gave the county the opportunity to make their opening remarks. In a preliminary hearing, the defense didn't present a case, but Devon would be given a chance to cross-examine the county's witnesses.

The representative for the county, a Mr. Herringbone, stood and solemnly addressed the jury.

"Gentleman of the jury, it is the position of Oak County that on the evening of the third of March, one thousand, eight hundred and ninety-three, Bennett Lawson Bennigan did, in fact, savagely render a weapon in the form of a rock against the person of Ethan James Bennigan and did, in turn, cause the death of the latter by trauma to the skull and subsequent drowning. Oak County will show throughout these proceedings that Bennett Bennigan did have motive in the form of financial grievances towards the deceased as well as the opportunity to act upon said grievances in order to cause the death of the deceased. As our first witness Oak County calls Miss Nancy A. Borden who was the first to come upon the murder scene."

Nancy rose shakily from her spot and timidly approached the witness bench, her head bent as she passed the jury box. She eased down upon the wooden bench and looked to the judge for the direction.

Judge Calvin gave her a welcoming smile and gestured to the attorney. "Mr. Herringbone, you may begin your examination of this witness."

Nodding, Mr. Herringbone scooted his rickety wooden chair backwards so forcefully Amelia thought it might collapse from the strain. He stood and walked to the center of the room, nodding politely to Nancy.

"Good Morning, Miss Borden. On behalf of Oak County, I would like to thank you for your cooperation in these proceedings today."

"You're very welcome, sir," Nancy almost whispered.

Poor thing, Amelia thought. *She is terrified.*

"Miss Borden, you are, in fact, employed by the Michael Sullivan family, is that correct?"

"Yes, sir."

"And how long have you been under their employ?"

"For nearly three years, sir."

"So you would say that the Sullivan's are fair employers?"

Nancy nodded enthusiastically. "Oh, yes, sir," she said and smiled at Amelia who returned the gesture. "They are the most wonderful folk to work for."

"That is indeed wonderful to hear, Miss Borden. Now, do you currently reside in the Sullivan home?"

"Yes, sir."

"And did you reside at the Sullivan home at the time of the night in question? In March of this year?"

"Yes, sir. I've lived at the house since I started workin' their 'bout three years ago."

"Excellent." Herringbone paused to jot down a note on his pad. "Were you raised in Moon Springs, Miss Borden?"

"Yes, sir."

"Does your family still reside there?"

"Yes. My mother is a seamstress in the village, and my father works at the stables, sir."

"Is that the only family you have in town?"

"Oh, no, sir! I have three brothers and two sisters that live there, too."

"What a wonderfully large family!"

"We're Catholic, sir," Nancy answered with nothing but complete honesty, but a low ripple of stifled laughter could be heard around the room.

"I see," noted Mr. Herringbone. "Miss Borden, can you tell me what you did at the Sullivan home on the night of March third of this year?"

"I attended to my duties, cleaning the family bedrooms and helping cook in the kitchen for dinner. They was having a party, you see—"

"—A party?" Mr. Herringbone interrupted.

"Yes, sir, a dinner party."

"Ah!" he exclaimed. "And do you know which guests attended the party?"

"I believe I do, sir. I believe it were the O'Briens, that is, Mr. and Mrs. They're Mr. Sullivan's relations, sir," she explained. "And Mr. Samuel and Miss May, of course, from the carriage house. Though… I suppose they're not really guests, what with 'em being family and all." She laughed nervously. "And then there was Mr. Ethan and Mr. Bennett."

"That would be the deceased, Ethan Bennigan, and his brother, Bennett Bennigan, the defendant, is that correct?"

"Yes, sir."

144

"Miss Borden, do you remember what the Sullivan family dinner party was served as a meal that evening?"

"Not precisely, sir, but I do believe there was chicken soup as a first course, and then there was bread pudding for dessert."

"Are you sure of those two items, Miss Borden?"

"Oh, yes, sir! Mighty sure! I made the bread pudding myself, you see." Nancy ducked her head shyly.

"You are indeed a lady with many talents, I presume," Mr. Herringbone said and smiled.

Nancy smiled hesitantly in return. Amelia knew he was just trying to keep her comfortable and investigate whether or not she would be a reliable witness.

"Thank you, sir."

"Miss Borden, were you on duty all night on March third?"

"No, sir. I was done for the night as soon as the coffee service began. It was my sister's birthday the next day, you see, and we was all going to spend the night with my folks so we'd have the chance to celebrate."

"Around what time would you say it was that you got off duty?"

"Around nine-thirty, I'd expect."

"And what did you do after that?"

"I went up to my room and packed an overnight bag and headed to town."

"May I ask, Miss Borden, did you leave through the front door of the house?"

"No, sir. That door is only for family and guests. I left through the back-kitchen door."

"I see, and where did you go after exiting the house?"

"I headed down the path in the woods towards the road to town."

"I'm curious, Miss Borden. Why did you not go down the driveway to meet up with the road?"

"Oh! That's the long way round sir. Everyone that works at the house knows the quickest way to town is through the woods."

"Is the path to town through the woods visibly marked?"

Nancy frowned in confusion. "I'm not sure what you mean, sir."

"Pardon me, I'll rephrase. Would someone that was a stranger to the Sullivan property know that the path was there?"

"No, I don't expect so."

"But all the staff and family were known to use that route to town?"

"Yes, sir."

"I see. Now what time did you set out for town?"

"Around midnight, sir."

"Did you see or hear anyone else moving along the path when you were walking?"

"No, sir."

"So you believed you were the only one on the path."

"Yes."

"And at what point did you find the deceased?"

"Just a little way in from the clearing. As I came round the bend, I seen his body laying down in the creek."

Amelia closed her eyes, willing away the image. It was a sight she knew she would never forget, and she had no desire to relive it now.

"I understand this is a difficult memory, Miss Borden, but can you please describe in detail what you saw at the scene?"

Nancy nodded somberly. "Yes. I came round the bend and saw what looked like a log sticking up from the creek. I didn't remember it being there earlier, so I thought maybe it had fallen recently and needed to be cleared. So I went up to it and then saw it was really a leg."

"Did you inspect further to identify the body?"

"At first I asked if whoever it was needed help. I thought maybe he was a drunk. That happens lots at night, see?"

"Yes, I can imagine. Go, on, please, Miss Borden."

"Well, he didn't answer, so I went up closer and looked over the edge of the creek bank and saw all that blood."

"And then what did you do?"

"Well, I screamed!"

"Did you see who it was down in the creek?"

"No, I didn't know who it was."

"Did you see anyone, anyone else at all on the path ahead of you at that time?"

147

"No, sir. No one. I looked, too. Thought maybe I'd catch who it was."

"But there was no one there?"

"No."

"Thank you, Miss Borden, that will be all."

The judge turned to Devon. "Would you like to cross-examine?"

Devon shook his head, which Amelia agreed with. Nancy had told nothing but the truth, and pushing her any further would threaten what few wits the poor girl had remaining at this point.

Mr. Herringbone addressed the jury. "We will now hear from the Sheriff of Moon Springs, Bryan Hastings. Subsequently, the county will call the fiancé of the deceased, Miss Amelia Sullivan, whose initial statements to authorities provided the basis for the defendant's arrest."

Amelia's gasp was audible as the room began to spin around her. She hadn't any idea they intended to call her as a witness. How could Devon have failed to mention this possibility? She could feel things going dark around her and knew she needed to get out of the room as quickly as possible. She stood and clumsily exited her seat, stumbling for the back of the room. The court officer guarding the entrance to the courtroom gave a slight nod as he opened the door for her.

Stepping into the main corridor, Amelia grabbed the arm of a bench directly outside the room and collapsed onto it in a very unladylike manner. Her shoulders heaved as she attempted to calm her breathing, and she wiped the perspiration that had sprung on her brow.

"I can't testify for the prosecution," she said aloud. "It could condemn him."

But of course, she saw no way out. If the prosecution called her, she would have to be sworn in or be in contempt of court. For the first time in her life, she saw no way out.

The door from the courtroom opened slightly, and a very concerned Devon slipped through and sat down beside her.

"I asked the judge for a brief recess to use the facilities," he said.

"Devon! Why didn't you—"

"—I had no idea, Amelia. The court is obligated to alert witnesses leading up to the preliminary hearing, but there is no time-specification, so they must have just mailed the letter today or yesterday while we were traveling."

"What are we going to do?" Amelia sighed.

"You'll do exactly as you are supposed to do," he said evenly. "You'll tell the truth. You and I both know Gabriel Desoto is to blame, so even if the prosecution doesn't bring him up, which they won't as it would jeopardize their case, I will be sure to cast doubt when I cross-examine you."

Amelia looked directly into Devon's eyes, and they were indeed confident and sure in his plan. She nodded, swallowing the bile which had escaped her stomach and willed its way to her throat.

"Now, you stay out here for a few moments and catch your breath. They won't call you this morning, certainly, so take your time." Devon stood and patted her hand as he opened the door to return to court.

"Thank you, Devon. I know Bennett is in good hands with you."

Devon didn't answer but nodded determinedly as he reentered the room.

Amelia let out another sigh and looked around. Perhaps a bit of fresh air would help calm her nerves. She'd only been to Smithton a few times and it had been years since her last visit. An exploratory stroll would distract her focus, albeit temporarily. She stood and walked to the entrance of the courthouse, descending the brick steps and making her way down the street towards the lovely park they had passed as they walked from the hotel that morning.

Purposely slowing her breaths to a normal level, she felt much better moving swiftly and purposely. She glanced in the window of the small dress shop and saw her reflection. She was ghostly pale and disheveled from her chaotic court exit. As she straightened her hairpins she noticed the man she had seen in court across the street, seemingly eyeing her.

She wondered *Why did he leave the courtroom?* as the man quickly looked away. *Perhaps he has errands to run. Perhaps he is another reporter heading out to get a start on his story*. Whatever the reason, the man turned and walked back down the street towards the courthouse, so she continued on towards her destination without another thought of him.

She stopped again to admire a cart of fresh flowers being peddled by a young girl.

Amelia smiled at her. "Good morning. How much for one bloom?"

The girl pulled a long white rose from her jug and held it up for Amelia to examine. "Ten cents, ma'am," she replied.

Taking a dime from her bag, Amelia pressed it into the girl's hand and took the rose. She brought it to her face to explore its scent.

"Thank you, it's lovely," she said as she turned to continue down the street towards the park. When she was at last directly across the wide street from the grassy garden that was her intended destination, she realized she couldn't get a clear view of the street because a large carriage was blocking her view, so she stepped back onto the boardwalk to walk around to the back of the carriage in order to cross when the door suddenly opened, slamming her in the arm.

"Oh my goodness, please excuse my rudeness," a low voice said as Amelia rubbing her tender elbow.

"It's fine," she insisted. "I'll be all right." She smiled as politely as possible in spite of the pain shooting up to her shoulder.

The man pointed behind her. "I believe I've made you lose your drawstring bag, ma'am."

Amelia turned to look when two muscular arms grabbed her around her waist and yanked her violently up into the carriage, banging her legs and head against the door again as they pulled her roughly inside. She tried to break free from the man's grip, kicking and trying to bite the arms that held her torso, but her efforts were fruitless. Another figure shoved a rancid cloth in front of her eyes. He yanked her head

151

backwards by her hair, tying a makeshift blindfold and sending her into darkness.

"Let me go! I'll give…I've got lots of money with me. Just let me out, and I'll leave the bag!"

"Sorry, Miss Sullivan," the second man said. "You'll not be able to return to court today."

Through a slight opening at the bottom of the blindfold she could see the pants and shoes of the speaker and recognized them immediately as belonging to the mysterious man from the courtroom. Shocked, the gravity of the situation sank in. "Dear, God," Amelia whispered.

This wasn't a random robbery. This was intentional. She was being kidnapped.

Chapter 10

Amelia tried again to reach for the carriage door, but the whole coach suddenly lurched forward, tossing her from the bench to the floor. The first man slid his arm under her waist and hoisted her back up onto the bench, wedging his body between hers and the door so she didn't dare attempt escape again.

Admitting defeat, at least temporarily, she collapsed against the bench and tried to smooth out her skirts, as if maintaining her appearance of decorum would make the situation better. One of the men took the opportunity to seize her wrists and wrap them tightly together in front of her in a splintering strand of twine.

"Is that really necessary?" she grumbled. "I can't see two inches in front of my face, and you're blocking my path. I obviously can't go anywhere."

"Yes, it's necessary," he drawled. "Mr. Desoto told us how feisty you might be and seems to me he was right."

Shrinking back into the corner in fear, Amelia now felt even more helpless than before. Of course it was Desoto who had orchestrated all this. If she didn't testify, there was no way for Devon to bring his name up in cross-examination, and she couldn't relate her firsthand knowledge of his horrendous character and vicious tendencies.

She tried to think of a decent retort for the man's insult so they wouldn't think she was intimidated by them, but she was too terrified to respond. Instead, she remained silent as the carriage picked up speed. The road grew increasingly bumpier as they moved ahead; she realized that they must be heading out of town to the roads that received less passage and maintenance. Not that it mattered. She was in an unfamiliar city. She had only been to Smithton a few times since childhood, and she had certainly never paid attention to the geography. If they traveled far enough from the courthouse, even if she did manage to escape, she could never find her way back to town alone.

The coach rolled ahead at a quick pace for what felt like thirty minutes or so before turning off onto an even bumpier road. Amelia braced herself as the compartment rocked back and forth over the tedious roots and stones she could almost visualize in her mind. It gave her something else to think about—trying to distinguish the type of road obstacle they traversed as they moved. Throughout the infinite journey she counted what she guessed to be fifty or so boulders they slowly drove over as well as hundreds of roots and what appeared to be one dead animal, judging from the grotesque odor that entered through the open slats in the thin carriage fabric.

Almost as abruptly as the carriage had begun to move in town, it came to a sudden stop. She heard the driver get down and walk around, unhitching the horses. Then she heard footsteps on what seemed to be wooden plank steps and a door creaking open.

"Where did you take me?" she demanded.

"That's none of your business, Miss Sullivan," said the man from the courthouse as he ripped the blindfold from her face.

"What do you mean it's none of my business? You've kidnapped me! I've at least the right to know where I am. It's not like I can tell anyone."

"Shut your mouth," the first man said as the carriage door opened to reveal a small log cabin directly in front of them.

The driver, an older man, just as scruffy and rough looking as the other two, walked ahead of them into the cabin. The man from the courthouse grabbed Amelia's arm and tugged her down out of the carriage.

"Come on now, hurry up," he said.

Amelia obeyed and walked as quickly as she could to follow the men up into the cabin. It was a dark, damp structure with two rooms that she could see. The main sitting room had a wood stove in the corner and a small table with four chairs that she doubted could actually hold the weight of a human being. Other than that, the room was bare. There was almost no natural light, save a tiny window in the corner by the stove, but the trees outside were so overgrown the sunlight barely broke through into the room. It felt much more like the prison it was than a home.

Not wanting to anger the men any further, Amelia stood still waiting for one of them to give her further directions, but that also proved to be a dangerous tactic. The driver stepped in again from the porch and shoved her towards the second room she hadn't yet glimpsed.

"Why you standing there, girl? Git in there!" he snarled.

Not even turning to look him in the eye, she nodded submissively and scooted to the doorway into the other room. It was not nearly as large as the main room, but it had a small mat on the floor stuffed with straw and covered with a burlap mat. A small wash basin sat on a foot stool under a solitary window much like the one in the other room, but at least this window did let in some more sunlight.

Not sure whether or not she was supposed to settle in this room or merely remain out of the way of the men, she turned back around and stood near the door, watching. The man from the courthouse had gone back outside to smoke a cigar on the porch, and she could hear the second man walking around the side of the house and opening what sounded like an ancient shed door.

"Staring at the door won't do you no good," said the driver. "You ain't going nowhere. Not till Mr. Desoto says to let you go."

Amelia's eyes snapped up. "Let me go? You mean—"

The man laughed. "Oh, you thought we were going to kill you?" He laughed again. "If we was going to kill you, we would have just done it. Not come all the way out here to this God-forsaken piece of trash." He gestured around at the cabin. "Naw. Our orders was just to keep you here for a few days until the hearing is over. Then I expect Mr. Desoto will let you go. Least that's what I was told." He nodded in the direction of the man from the courthouse who was still sitting out on the front steps. Amelia had decided he must be in charge of this operation.

She turned and looked back to the mat on the floor as another thought, almost more horrifying than the threat of death, suddenly took hold and made her want to throw up. Sensing what she feared, the man laughed again.

"Oh, don't worry about none of that, neither. Our orders are to not touch you at all, just to keep you here and keep you quiet until the trial is over. Don't get your skirts in a knot."

"Charlie!" the man on the porch suddenly looked over his shoulder at her and the driver.

"Yeah, Mac?" the driver responded.

"Cut that rope off her hands. I'm getting hungry.

Amelia turned to Charlie and looked down at her throbbing wrists hopefully. It would feel so much better to have the use of her hands again.

Charlie grunted an unintelligible response, went to the stove, and took the pot off the top. He opened the lid to reveal a rudimentary set of kitchen utensils, including a rusted knife. Amelia held up her hands as he crossed back over to her, and he sawed off the twine. Rubbing the blisters that covered each arm, she looked him in the eyes gratefully and nodded. She couldn't bear to let herself thank one of the men who had kidnapped her, but she really was so glad to get her arms unbound.

She turned to walk back into the bedroom, but Charlie asked, "Where do you think you're going?"

Frowning in confusion, she said, "I thought I might rest for a bit. It *has* been a bit of a challenging afternoon."

"I don't think so," Charlie said. "Didn't you hear Mac? We're hungry."

"What do you expect me to do about that?"

"What ya think, woman? Make us some food!"

Amelia's arms dropped down by her sides as she looked around the room. "With what?"

"With whatever we got! Didn't your momma teach you nothing?"

Scoffing, she folded her arms. "So, just because I'm a woman, I should automatically be an excellent cook? No wonder the only job you can find is as Desoto's hired thug. Didn't *your* momma teach you manners?"

Jaw dropping in amusement, Charlie stood up straighter. "Well, well, we do have ourselves a smart one, Mac!" he called outside.

The sound of Mac jumping to his feet and stomping towards the front door brought Amelia back to reality, and she nodded toward the woods. "If you let me go look for something edible outside, I can come up with something. But you'll need to get me a large pot of boiling water."

Mac nodded to Charlie who obediently took the pot outside and headed down to the tiny creek flowing behind the house. He pointed in the opposite direction to the woods across from the cabin.

"There's an old farm over in that field. You can find something over there."

Amelia did see, through the dense stand of pines, a clearing and what looked to be a dilapidated farmhouse leaning precariously to the right. Amelia turned back and looked at him incredulously. "That place looks like it's been abandoned for at least a year. And you think I'll 'find' something there? Do you

158

know anything about farming? There's a reason farmers are slaves to the calendar and the weather. They have to plant their crops every year, and the weather has to be perfect, or there is no crop! I can't just walk over to some building that 'used' to be a farm and expect there to be food."

He turned and walked into the cabin and reached up over the doorway. He pulled down a rifle Amelia hadn't seen before. She backed away from the door and put her hands up in front of her face.

"Please, don't! I'm sorry. I'm sure I'll find something."

Mac grunted and pointed the barrel of the gun towards the woods. "Get going. I can see you from here. If you try to run, I'll just shoot you. And don't think I can't shoot through those trees. I was a marksman in the war for the Confederacy. Once shot a man's head clean off from two hundred feet."

Shuddering, Amelia didn't bother to reply. She did as she was told and walked down the steps across the path towards the farmhouse. It took her only a few minutes to get to where the house stood; it looked so derelict she was certain it had been abandoned several years ago.

Just to be sure, she called out a timid, "Hello?" and, not hearing a response, she began looking around for a garden or nearby crop field where she could search for some food. On the left side of the house there was nothing but some old shrubs and broken glass where the windows had collapsed under the pressure of the sagging second story. She decided to try around the back of the house, but as she went to step around the corner, a pop as loud as a thunder clap exploded through the air from the direction of the cabin.

She fell to the ground and covered her head, not daring to even raise it to confirm that the noise had come from Mac. For the first time that whole day she was near tears. She'd never been shot at before, and she had to wonder if this raw, oppressive fear is what Ethan had been feeling when he was murdered.

A rustling in the trees behind her finally forced her to turn her head in the direction of where the shot had come from. She was relieved to see Charlie, not Mac, walking towards her. She was even more grateful that he didn't have a gun with him.

"Get up, you skittish little thing," he ordered.

Standing and brushing off her skirts, Amelia yanked her head in the direction of the cabin. "What was he thinking?"

"He was thinking you were fixing to escape."

"Well. He was thinking wrong. I was just looking for some food, like he asked me to do."

"That's what I figured. So I told him I'd come keep an eye on you so he doesn't have to go drawing any more attention to us. Lord knows they're probably out looking for you by now. Shooting a gun is just plain stupid if you ask me, especially if he plans to miss."

He bent to pick up a piece of straw out of a bale that was still roped next to the front porch of the house. Putting it in his mouth, he mumbled, "All right. Let's get to work."

Turning to look one more time back at the cabin and seeing that Mac was no longer on the front porch, Amelia breathed a small sigh of relief. He hadn't been kidding when he said he would shoot her, but she suspected the first one had just been a warning shot. If she made a mistake like that again, she was sure he would not hesitate to kill her.

They walked to her original destination—the back of the house—and Amelia was delighted to find two huge blackberry bushes tucked against the wall. It was still a bit early for blackberries, but she saw that several were ripe enough to be edible but tart and immediately began searching for something to store them in.

Charlie saw what she was after and pointed back around the front of the house.

"I think there's a bucket on the porch. I'll go fetch it."

This time she did allow herself to say a small "thank you" in return.

At least he's being marginally helpful, she thought.

By the time Charlie came back around the house she had already collected a few handfuls of berries for the bucket. She hurriedly gathered a few more fistfuls, careful to leave some for tomorrow in the event she would need them, although she hoped beyond hope she wouldn't.

Hooking the bucket over the crook of her arm, Amelia continued around to the far side of the house she hadn't yet explored and approached a small patch of grass that looked different from the rest of the yard.

"We can't eat that. Them's just weeds," Charlie complained.

"Be patient," Amelia said, shaking her head and dropping to her knees. She got down very close to the grass and yanked at a long stalk sticking out of the dirt. "Aha! See? It's not just weeds!" She turned triumphantly to show Charlie.

"Well, what is it then?" he asked skeptically. "Sure looks like a weed to me."

She sat back on her heels, grateful for the hours she'd spent out in the fields with Uncle Patrick when she was a little girl. She put the long stalk of the plant in her mouth and took a big bite, savoring the tangy juice of the plant. She looked up at Charlie and smiled. "It's a leek."

"A leek? Never heard of it."

"Well, I have, and I happen to know that leeks make an excellent soup. Now, help me pull all the plants that look like this. It's fine if we gather them all today. The ones we don't use will keep in the cabin for a few days for sure, considering how damp and cool it is in there."

Obliging, Charlie knelt down beside her and began to pull up the leeks, more than three dozen in all. After they were sure they'd gotten every last one, Amelia gathered them up in her arms, and they walked back to the cabin.

As they climbed the stairs and entered the main room, Amelia could see the water she'd requested already boiling on the stove and three more straw mats laid out along the front wall next to the door. The other man, whose name she still didn't know, was busy stuffing straw in the last one. Apparently, they would all be sharing the cabin that night.

Dear God, please don't let Mother hear about this. She'd faint dead away for sure. But, since she had already been assured by Charlie that no harm would come to her unless Mac thought she was trying to escape again, she didn't really mind the fact that they would be blocking the door. She'd already determined she wouldn't know which direction to go if she ran, so she certainly wouldn't be attempting to escape in the middle of the night.

She set the bucket of berries on the table, and all three men immediately began helping themselves. Purple juice running down his mouth, Mac looked at the other food she'd brought. "What in the Sam Hill is that?"

"It's a leek," Charlie said, knowingly. "And I've been told it makes delicious soup."

Amelia nearly laughed out loud at his haughtiness. If they had met under different circumstances, she would have been very fond of Charlie. She took the leeks and brushed as much dirt off as she could with her skirt, and then threw half of them into the boiling water.

She turned back around to face the men. "I'm afraid it will be a very unfulfilling soup, as all we have are leeks. Of course, if I had some meat of some sort, it would be much hardier."

Mac looked at Charlie and nodded towards the gun. Charlie grabbed the rifle and headed out the door. It wasn't more than ten minutes later when Amelia heard a single shot, followed by the sound of Charlie's voice, calling, "Jimmie! Bring me a knife so I can skin this varmint!"

Fixing her eyes on Jimmie, Amelia smiled and said, "Please don't remove anything but the fur, and intestines, if you don't mind. A lean rabbit leaves very little potential for a good broth." She turned back to the pot and moved it temporarily off the fire to wait for the rabbit, which arrived on a bloodied, rusted tin plate several minutes later. She gestured to the pot, and Jimmie let the meat slide in next to the leeks; then, using her skirt as protection for her hands, she moved the pot back onto the open flame and covered the lid, allowing the rabbit and leek to stew harmoniously.

She flopped down in the chair closest to the stove and stared at the pot, finding the whole process of waiting for the soup terribly boring after the excitement of the rest of the day. She noticed that the already dim light coming in from the window was quickly fading. Devon would have most certainly realized she was missing by now and not just fearful of testifying, but, beyond that, she didn't have any idea what would happen next. Her kidnappers had to have turned onto at least five different roads during their journey out to the cabin. There was no way Devon would know where to look for her easily. She had to pray they would find her before Desoto changed his mind and decided he didn't need her alive anymore.

Feeling the urgency of her predicament tightening in her chest, she glanced around the room. Charlie sat propped in the corner with his hat down over his eyes. Jimmie picked at remnants of his last meal in his teeth with a piece of straw. *Fine specimens of creation,* she thought. Mac stood tall in the open doorway, looking up and down the road. Assuming he was looking out for passing traffic and deciding he was the responsible one among the bunch, she addressed him. "Might I be able to take a walk while we wait for the soup to finish? I am dreadfully sore from the rough journey today."

Mac frowned and then nodded. "You can go, but stay on this side of the creek. Jimmie here will keep an eye on you from the porch to make sure you don't try nothing funny."

Gruffly obeying Mac's orders, Jimmie followed Amelia out onto the front porch and sat on the steps as she slowly made her way down and out into the yard. As she stepped over roots and fallen branches towards the creek, she took the opportunity to examine the window of her room to see how high it was off the ground, just in case. Thankfully she guessed the sill to be only about seven or eight feet off the ground, and the window was definitely wide enough for her to squeeze through if she needed to.

Sensing Jimmie's watchful eyes on her every move, Amelia made it down to the water and sat down on a large rock. Caring little how unladylike she appeared at the moment, she slid off her stockings and shoes, which were both horridly muddy after her journey to the old farm, and dipped her toes in the water. Although it was bitterly cold, at the same time it soothed her aching feet. She submerged them completely, wiggling her joints liberally.

Looking back at her shoes and stockings, Amelia suddenly had the urge to clean them, even though it would mean being barefoot during dinner. Frankly, she didn't care what the kidnappers thought of her decency and manners, and it seemed like the only thing she could do under her own volition at the moment, so she went ahead with it. After her footwear and her own feet were thoroughly scrubbed, she gathered everything back up, hiked up her skirts and climbed back up the shallow bank to check on the soup. Jimmie raised his eyebrows in amusement at the sight of her bare feet but didn't say anything. She stepped inside and laid her stockings over the handle of one of the extra pots to dry.

Despite her circumstances, she was starving, and the stew smelled wonderful. She could find only two tin bowls, so she spooned out a helping for Mac and Jimmie first, willing to tempt Charlie's patience instead of that of the others, and waited for them to eat.

Thankfully, the men seemed just as hungry as she was, so both were finished quickly, turning over their bowls to Charlie and Amelia to eat the second round. After scooping out some stew for Charlie, Amelia filled up her own bowl, then carried it into the other room. Thankfully none of the men complained about her exit, and in solitude she would be able to savor the first meal she'd had in nearly twelve hours.

Gingerly, she lowered herself onto the mat, realizing for the first time that her ribs were quite bruised from her struggle with Mac and Jimmie. Shifting to a different position, she set the bowl onto the stool beside the bed and stretched her legs out in front of her. As hungry as she was, she couldn't bring herself to take the first bite.

She shook her head. *Okay, Amelia. Don't lose your mind now. Dying of starvation before Devon finds you would be ridiculous.*

She finally forced the spoon to her mouth. She was so hungry, it tasted delicious, and she was able to empty the entire contents of the bowl. Exhaustion finally took over, and she didn't bother to take the bowl out to the stove or retrieve her stockings. Instead, she curled up into as tight a ball as she could to try to stay warm. She heard the kidnappers out in the other room joking and enjoying the warmth of the stove, but she hardly felt the need to call out *goodnight* and rolled over to face the wall.

Even though she was physically more tired than she'd ever been in her life, she struggled to fall asleep. Every time she came close, she'd hear a cough or grunt in the other room, and reality would come throttling back to stare her in the face. She'd been in several perilous situations in her life, most often brought on by her own stupidity or lack of judgment, but this one far surpassed any of those. She tried to devise a plan for how she would escape in the morning, but each method she thought of required her to be left alone, and she knew the men would never do that.

Desoto's men had probably scouted out this building, which she could only assume was a seasonal laborer's cabin or a hunting shack, because of its relative isolation. Her only real hope was that the owners would find some reason to stop by unexpectedly. Judging by the lack of furniture in the house, she doubted there was any chance of that occurring.

167

A screech resonated through the window, and she nearly jumped out of her skin before realizing it was just an owl. She hugged herself again and tried to slow her rapid breathing. She turned back to face the outer room's door. As much as she loathed the men on the other side, she found it slightly comforting to know she wasn't completely alone in those woods.

Chapter 11

Leaves rustling outside the window aroused Amelia from her fitful sleep as soon as the sun came up. Half of her had expected to wake up realizing the previous day had been a nightmare, but the fact that her fiancé had been murdered months before reminded her that real life could be worse than a nightmare. Urging her throbbing torso to roll over with her to face the room, she rubbed her eyes and peered through the door frame and into the kitchen. She could see all three men were still sound asleep on their mats. She sat up quietly and tiptoed out of the bed and into the room where they were to retrieve her stockings and shoes. Despite the fact that it was July, the morning air was surprisingly crisp, and the stockings which had hung over the stove fire all night were cozy on her swollen feet.

Afraid to wake the sleeping men, she sat quietly on the chair closest to the stove. With nothing to read and no one to talk to, and too tired to move, she sat and listened to the birds and animals outside the cabin. To distract herself from thinking, she tried to identify separate birds before the men awoke. The first was simple—a woodpecker busy searching out insects on a nearby tree. Next, she heard the distinctive sound of a chickadee, but whether it was in a tree or on the ground hunting summer seeds, she didn't know. A horrific squealing from just beyond the direction of the creek followed by a fluttering of wings and rustling of branches made her suspect a falcon had found himself breakfast.

Poor little thing. Life is sometimes so unfair.

Before she could listen for a fourth bird, another sound caught her attention—wagon wheels bumping down the road. Senses alerted, she quickly considered her options. She could attempt to jump over Mac, open the door, shout for help, but she'd have to fight against his weight which was resting squarely on the only exit from the cabin. Or, she could call out for help from the window and pray that whoever was on the wagon could hear her over the sound of the road and also see her through the dense overgrowth of the trees on that side of the cabin. Either way, she knew if she failed in her attempt at signaling help, it was possible the men would be angry and kill her to end their troubles. If only she had more time to think it through, but she knew her opportunity would pass quickly.

Obeying her instincts, she scrambled over to the window and leaned her head out to yell, but the wagon suddenly stopped outside the cabin instead of passing. A new sense of fear engulfed her as she saw Gabriel Desoto, the only passenger, jump down from the driver's seat and stride towards the front steps. Pulling her head inside quickly, she prayed he hadn't glimpsed her plotting an escape attempt. Meanwhile, she picked up a pot and placed it over the fire on the stove.

Gabriel attempted to come inside, but when he tried, the door hit Mac's shoulder. Shouting in protest he jumped to his feet, looking at Amelia in confusion.

She didn't bother to enlighten him and instead waited for Desoto to push his way into the room.

"Of all the lazy…" Gabriel growled, kicking Charlie in the ribs. Charlie rolled over in self-defense onto Jimmie.

"What the devil?" yelped Jimmie. He fell silent immediately when he saw his boss.

"Good Morning, Mr. Desoto," Charlie said, nodding respectfully as he rose to his feet. Again, Amelia found herself wishing they could have met under different circumstances. He was too well-mannered to work for such a louse.

"How in the world am I supposed to expect— and *pay*—you to guard her when she's walking freely around the house while you three are sleeping the day away?" Gabriel shouted.

Mac looked out the front door and shrugged. "Can't be more than seven in the morning, Boss. Besides, I was blocking the door. She couldn't get out."

Gabriel gave him a sideways glance before he turned to stare at Amelia coldly, "Oh really? I saw her halfway out the window when I pulled up just now. I'd say you're lucky I wasn't just a few minutes later. It would have been your bodies I was burying instead of hers."

Gasping, Amelia took several steps backwards until she slammed into the wall under the kitchen window.

"What do you mean?" she cried. "Charlie said his orders were to leave me unharmed!"

"They were," Desoto replied, "as long as you followed the rules."

171

"I didn't break any of your ridiculous rules. Mac nearly shot my head off yesterday when I was trying to get food for us to eat, so you can trust that I learned my lesson. Is it against the rules to get fresh air? I couldn't walk onto the porch, so I opened the window." Looking in the direction of the other men, she continued mounting her defense, however untrue. "Sleeping in a space smaller than my washroom with these three makes a girl yearn for clean air. Really, Gabriel, you should allow your thugs to bathe once in a while."

Amelia attempted to maintain a brave face so he wouldn't be able to see how afraid she was, but she didn't know how much longer she could keep up her ruse. She believed he was ready to kill her if he guessed she was lying about the window.

Miraculously, Charlie spoke up in her defense. "She's right, boss. She ain't broken any of our rules, and she made us dinner. I reckon she was doing just as she said she was. She ain't lied to us once since we got her here."

Amelia hoped her eyes told the story of her gratefulness to Charlie as she nodded.

Taking a timid step away from the wall near the the stove, she spied the pot. Looking down at the pot, she noticed it was nearly boiling now, and she tried to think of something else to say. *I have to make him think I'm being cooperative and bide my time until Devon can find me. I know he'll find me. He must.*

She spied some herbal plants outside the window and spoke up, trying to distract them from thoughts. "I could brew some tea and we could eat the berries I found before. Or would you like to show some decency and take me back to town? You could do that. You could take me back, admit you made a mistake, and leave." She knew she was babbling, but she couldn't seem to stop. The terror began to build as she envisioned the future. "Just go away somewhere. Just go away and promise you won't return. I promise never to tell the authorities who kidnapped me."

"Ha! I'm afraid I'll have to decline, Miss Sullivan," he smirked. "You're not in the position to be making suggestions right now, so I'd keep your mouth shut if I were you."

Amelia looked down at the floor. Of course, she had known it wouldn't be that easy, but she needed to keep him talking so he wouldn't get other ideas. She looked back up.

"Might I at least get the herbs for the tea, then, Mr. Desoto? It seems like you might be staying with us for a while. It would be nice to have something besides boiling water to drink for breakfast, at least…ahem… in my opinion."

The back of his hand hit her cheek.

"You piece of trash! I told you to shut up!"

Amelia looked up at him, shocked, as she put a hand to her cheek. It stung ferociously. "I'm sorry," she winced. But he leaned over her, gripping her arms in his course hands.

"Please, stop!" she cried out in pain. He dug his fingers into her arms and shoved her down onto one of the chairs. Turning to Mac, he ordered him to fetch a rope. He furiously wound the rope tightly around her chest and the chair several times but did not tie her arms or legs. Still, she felt the indignation and knew she would not be able to move easily.

She squeezed her eyes closed and managed a quiet, "God, please," before he ripped the handkerchief out of his pocket and gagged her with it.

Gabriel slapped her across the other cheek. "Darling," he drawled, mockingly, "haven't you learned by now that God doesn't care about the Sullivan family? You're nothing but a group of pompous thieves hiding behind your fancy clothes and soirees. You should know your God doesn't take kindly to thievery"

Amelia tilted her head forward, spit the gag out of her mouth and looked up at him in anger. "I would swear on my grandmother's grave you can't remember a word of anything you heard in Sunday school! And what do you mean calling my family thieves? We didn't take anything from you!"

"Really?" he mused. "Then please, your ladyship, do explain why it is that I'm still without the thousands of dollars your fiancé owed me when he died."

Amelia rolled her head back in exasperation. "We've been over this, Gabriel!" Her desire to use proper formalities vanished the moment he struck her. "We don't owe you anything. I wasn't married to Ethan. I have no access to his money! Bennett could have gotten it for you, but you had him framed for murder!"

"I didn't frame him. It was your nosiness that got him arrested. And who knows, he might have done it!"

"We both know he didn't."

"Well, then, when the jury decides not to prosecute him, he'll be free to pay me back. Then I'll gladly leave."

"Bennett has paid enough!" she cried. "He's been in prison four months for something he didn't do. He hasn't been able to properly grieve. He's never even met his nephew. He doesn't owe you a dime. Besides, you'll never convince me it wasn't you who killed Ethan."

"You ridiculous woman! I told you—your fiancé's ignorance has nearly ruined my entire business. I've lost prospects in other cities. I've lost clients. I've wasted hours cozying up to your pathetic excuse for a sister and haven't gained back a dime of what I'm owed."

"Do *not* talk about my sister that way!" Amelia screamed. Gabriel stood up to strike her again, but she mustered all her strength, reared up even tied to the chair and kneed him in the groin when he was close enough.

Gabriel writhed in pain and surprise at her retaliation but recovered quickly and snatched one of the rusty knives from the bowl, grabbed her hair, and yanked her head backwards till she thought her neck was going to snap. Staring up at the ceiling now with his face only inches from hers, she could smell tobacco on his breath as he huffed over her mouth.

"Listen to me carefully, Miss Sullivan." His voice was a hoarse whisper. "Do not try anything like that again, or I will slit your throat."

Eyes wide, she did her best to nod. He snapped her head back up and walked back around the chair, lowering his head down until his face was almost touching hers again.

"Let me tell you how this is going to work," he began. "My boys are going to keep you here until all of the testimonies are given at the hearing. Lucky for you, the sheriff didn't complete his yesterday, so you've still got today."

He stood and crossed the room to stand in the corner. "If, by some miracle, they let Bennett go, I'll drive you back to Moon Springs where you and Bennett will get me my money. Then I'll leave, and you'll never hear from me again." Sensing her confusion, he chuckled. "And don't even think about going to the authorities because you wouldn't believe how many of them are on my payroll. I'll have Bennett back in prison, for good, within a day."

Amelia shuddered when she saw the truth of it in his eyes.

"If," he continued, "they do decide to take Bennett to a full trial, I'll drive you back to your home, and you will persuade your father to give me the money, or I promise you, Bennett will never make it to trial alive."

"What makes you think my father has that kind of money?"

"You mean you don't know? It was your father who gave Ethan the extra money he added to his initial investment in Savannah. If he had that money before, he has it now. Ethan may have been an ignorant business man, but your father is no fool. He probably

176

didn't invest a year's worth of profit with Ethan. I know men like him. He has plenty of money handy if the cause is worthy enough," Gabriel said, laughing, "and I'd wager Bennett's life would fall under that category, wouldn't you?"

Amelia couldn't believe what she was hearing. Her father? It had all been *his* money? That didn't make any sense. She and Devon had looked at the books together. There were at least half a dozen names on that list. Unless, he had made the investments under pseudonyms to keep it from someone. Mother? May? She had no idea, but, at the moment it didn't matter. She knew Gabriel was right. Her father had much more money than Ethan had lost in Savannah, and he *would* pay to save any life, especially Bennett's.

She looked back at Desoto. "If that's your plan, then why tie me up? Why did you take me in the first place? Both plans end with you taking me home."

He shrugged. "I kidnapped you so that you wouldn't try to bring my good name into question trying to exonerate Bennett." Amelia scoffed at his ignorance. "I tied you up," Gabriel growled, "because you angered me. I don't take kindly to people who anger me."

"Like you didn't take kindly to Ethan refusing to repay you before you killed him?" She was desperate now for answers. She had to know, even if it meant angering him further. She braced herself for another blow, but it never came.

"You truly believe I did it, don't you?" Gabriel finally asked.

And at that moment, after four months of wondering, Amelia realized that he hadn't. Sure, he was a monster of a businessman, a kidnapper, and probably a murderer at some other time, but thinking back to all of her encounters with him, she recalled that the only time he had seemed truly shocked and sincere was when she had accused him of killing Ethan. But she didn't want to give him the satisfaction of admitting she'd been wrong. She focused her gaze on the window and remained silent because, murderer or not, he had still kidnapped and assaulted her.

Gabriel turned around and approached the porch where the other men had escaped during their argument, and, suddenly, the barrel of a shotgun appeared in the doorway at his eye level. She watched him grab for the gun above the door, but before he could get it, the wielder of the shotgun swung into view, moving the gun down to poke right into Desoto's chest.

"Back up into the house. Now!"

Desoto obeyed, raising his hands submissively in the air and stepping backwards into the cabin.

"Devon!" Amelia cried, never more grateful to see a familiar face in her entire life.

Suddenly, three more armed men, all in uniform, burst into the room, quickly subduing Gabriel and tying his hands behind his back. Amelia watched as they dragged him out of the cabin and down the steps and then marched away down the road.

Devon rushed to Amelia's side.Confusion clouded her eyes while he explained, "We had to leave the wagons down the road so they wouldn't hear us approaching. There are two more officers outside holding the other men." Grabbing the knife from the bowl, he cautioned her to be still as he carefully sawed through the rope that had secured her so tightly to the chair. She thrust her body forward. Soon her arms were loose, and within minutes he had released her completely from her bondage. She tried to stand, but when she rose, her head throbbed, and she had to sit back down.

Devon grabbed a chair and sat down in front of Amelia. As she rubbed her aching temples, he reached a hand toward her face. She recoiled sharply and began to apologize, but he slowly put his finger to her lips.

"Millie. It's fine. I shouldn't have reached for you so suddenly. It's just…your face."

Realizing for the first time that both of her eyes were nearly swollen shut, she felt the tears stinging her wounds as she began to weep.

Devon reached for her and silently pulled her across the space separating them until she was completely wrapped in his arms. She buried her face in his shoulder as he gently stroked the back of her head, trying clumsily to smooth back her matted and tear-stained hair from in front of her eyes. Whimpering, she held on to his sleeves not wanting to be released from the strength and safety of his grasp.

After several minutes, she sat back and looked up at him. "Thank you," she managed to whisper through her shivering.

But she saw he wasn't looking at her. She followed his gaze to the floor where the kidnappers' mats were still strewn across the ground. His mouth twisted fiercely as he looked into her eyes.

"Amelia… Did any of those men…"

She saw him trying to find the appropriate words. "No. They didn't touch me."

She realized how ridiculous that sounded, considering how swollen her face was, so she clarified. "They didn't touch me, until today. But even then, what you see is the extent of it."

His shoulders relaxed, and his arms, which had tightened around her protectively, loosened. He leaned his forehead against hers, cupped her cheeks in his hands, and moaned in relief. Suddenly sensing how intimately they were entwined as she was practically on his lap, she quickly retreated to her seat on the chair where she'd been tied, but as she leaned back into the seat she doubled over in pain.

"What is it?" Devon asked.

Amelia ran her hands along her side. "I think maybe I have a broken rib. From when they took me yesterday," she explained.

He stared out the door to where the uniformed deputies were loading all four men into a police wagon. "I hope they rot in prison," he said with venom.

"Me, too," Amelia agreed.

They watched in silence as the wagon turned around and headed back toward town. Then Devon carefully helped Amelia to her feet and they made their way down the porch stairs and climbed into the wagon Desoto had arrived in earlier that morning. The covered carriage would have been much more comfortable, but Amelia couldn't bring herself to sit in it after the trauma of the previous day. She opted for Gabriel's simpler wagon instead.

As Devon hitched the horses up and climbed into the seat next to her, Amelia realized she was extremely hungry and began to nibble on the berries she'd kept in her skirt pocket the night before. They were mashed up and stained her fingers but tasted fabulous after her ordeal.

They rode in silence for several minutes as Amelia surveyed the roads down which she had traveled with the kidnappers. She realized she indeed had no idea where they'd taken her—not even a general guess as to the direction. Had she tried to escape, she would have been terribly lost and likely have died from exposure before finding any signs of civilization.

The thought prompted her to break the silence Devon had been keeping so respectfully. "Devon, how did you find me so quickly?"

He detailed the events of the previous day after she'd been taken. When she hadn't returned by the break at lunchtime, Devon had grown concerned. When he checked in with the hotel and had been told she hadn't been there either, he knew something had gone horribly awry. He went down the street between the hotel and the courthouse, asking everyone if they had seen her.

He'd come across the young girl who had been selling flowers. When questioned, she recalled she had sold a rose to a lady fitting her description and told him which direction she'd seen her go. When he followed the girl's instructions and strode across from the park, he found the rose along the ridge of the road and realized Amelia had been taken.

"How did you know who had done it?"

He shook his head. "I didn't. But I knew where to start. The only people in town who would know who you were would have been at the courthouse. I deduced you had been followed from there. So I went back to the courthouse, and when lunch break was over, I searched the room to see who hadn't returned. I noticed one man was absent, but another man whom I'd seen that morning was still there. So, I asked the judge for a recess until this morning, and I followed the man. Thankfully, he led me to a saloon where he sat down next to none other than Gabriel Desoto. At that point, I realized it was Desoto who had taken you, so I stayed out of sight until he returned to his hotel. Then I went to the sheriff's office and explained what I believed had happened to you. The sheriff posted a guard in the hotel entrance last night and then alerted us when Desoto left this morning. Just as I'd hoped, he led us straight to you. We had to stay back pretty far from his wagon so he wouldn't grow suspicious, but, thankfully, it rained a bit last night so we were able to follow the freshest tracks on the road."

Amelia smiled in spite of herself. "Devon, that was simply brilliant! I knew you would be looking for me, but I figured it would take at least a week to find me! I don't know how I would have survived that." She turned away, ashamed at the tears that had again clouded her eyes, but Devon put his hand on top of hers.

"Don't think about that now, Millie. It's over. And I swear, I won't ever let anything like that happen to you again."

Chapter 12

After a very long nap in her hotel room with sheriff's deputies on guard outside, just in case, Amelia emerged in the late afternoon feeling refreshed but still very sore from the bruises Desoto and his men had inflicted. She made her way down the hallway to find a maid and request a hot bath be drawn in her room. Finding no one on her floor, she descended the stairs down onto the main floor to ask the concierge and saw a familiar silhouette checking in at the front desk.

"Adele!" she cried.

Her sister turned and ran to her, nearly knocking her over from the enthusiasm of her embrace.

"Careful! I'm a bit sore there, "Amelia cautioned.

Adele leaned back and ran her hands gently over Amelia's face. "I'm just sick over what that monster did to you. Devon told me everything when he met my coach just now."

After making their request at the counter for a hot bath, Amelia slipped her arm through her sister's and gingerly climbed back up the stairs, pausing a few times to catch her breath from the pain in her side. When they entered the room, Adele took the pin out of her hat and set the red velvet garment on the desk. Then she joined Amelia on the settee.

"How did you get here so quickly?" Amelia asked.

"Devon telegrammed us yesterday afternoon to say you'd gone missing, and I begged Father and

184

Mother to let me come help look for you. They agreed to let me come first this morning. Jeffrey got lost on the way, or we would have been here much sooner, but it still only took a few hours. I was so relieved that Devon saw us coming and was able to head off the coach and tell us he'd found you."

Amelia leaned her head onto Adele's shoulder, and the sisters sat in contented silence for several minutes until a soft knock at the door announced the maid with the steaming pitchers of hot water.

Taking off her clothes was more difficult than Amelia had imagined it would be, so Adele assisted in the task, taking great care not to touch her sister's darkening wounds. Amelia hadn't taken off her chemise when she'd arrived back at the hotel that morning since she had been so tired, so when Adele slid it off, she gasped in horror. Wide purple streaks were striped across Amelia's ribcage and chest, including the outline of several handprints smattered all over the flesh normally covered by her bodice.

"Amelia! What did they do to you?"

Amelia turned around and gave her sister another reassuring hug. "Don't worry. It's not what you think. I think they just broke a few ribs when they were pulling me into the carriage yesterday."

Not believing her, Adele leaned in to examine the bruises more closely. "Do you swear? You're not just trying to protect me? Because you could tell me, Millie. I promise I'm brave enough. In fact, I want to know every detail of what happened to you, so you don't have to remember it alone."

Grasping her sister's hands in hers, Amelia thought back to how Gabriel had insulted Adele and thanked God he'd been completely wrong. Most proper ladies wouldn't want to know anything of the sort, but she knew her sister meant every word.

"I promise, Adele. They didn't take advantage of me in that way. Although they weren't the gentlest of creatures either," she winced as she bent to pick up her handkerchief from the floor.

Adele helped Amelia ease into the bath the maid had prepared. She took great care in rinsing out Amelia's hair, sponging her back and face and then tieing her hair up into a simple French twist upon Amelia's exit from the tub.

Grabbing a dress from Amelia's travel trunk, she held it up for approval. Amelia nodded, "That one is fine. It's loose and comfortable," she said and began to chuckle.

"What's so funny?"

"I just realized that having broken and bruised ribs means mother can't try to make me wear a corset for at least a month. A blessing in disguise."

Adele was not amused. She helped Amela put on her light satin gown and then changed out of her travel clothes.

The sisters headed downstairs to the lobby where they met Devon, who had just returned from visiting Bennett in the prison.

"Excellent timing, ladies. Amelia, I need to speak with you regarding your testimony if you feel up for it. Of course, I understand if you're not. You've been through so much."

Amelia held up her hand in protest. "No, of course, Devon! I'm absolutely ready to discuss the case. I'm determined to help Bennett in any way that I can."

Amelia gestured toward a small table in the corner near the unused fireplace and led the three to some seats around it. They ordered tea and biscuits from the small hotel restaurant. While they waited for their food, Amelia filled Devon and Adele in on her conclusion that Desoto really did not have anything to do with Ethan's death—a fact she had not shared with either of them since her rescue. Neither looked convinced, but upon Amelia's insistence, they both saw the merits of Desoto's arguments and Amelia's instinct that, on that fact alone, he had been completely truthful.

"Well, if he didn't do it, he'll still be imprisoned for kidnapping you, and we, at least, don't have to worry about him persisting in trying to get money from the family, but I still wish we knew who did it," Devon concluded.

"Agreed," said Adele. "If it wasn't Bennett, and it wasn't Desoto, then who was it?"

A thought flashed through Amelia's mind, but she quickly willed it away, deeming it preposterous. But the moment was not lost on Adele.

"What is it, Millie? I can tell something's bothering you."

Amelia glanced back and forth between the two reluctantly, unwilling to reveal her father's financial contributions to Ethan before she had a chance to process the implications herself. "I'm fine, really. Just tired. It hasn't been the easiest few days, you know."

Guilt clouded Adele's face. "Oh, of course. I'm so sorry Millie. I didn't mean to accuse."

Amelia smiled warmly, assuring her sister all was well. She turned back to Devon. "Now, tell me what transpired in court yesterday after I...left."

Devon nodded and pulled a small notebook from his pocket.

"Honestly, it hasn't been going well. The state's case against Bennett is a strong one. His knowledge of Ethan's business dealings and, more specifically, his failures and their effects on the Bennigan family affairs as a whole is a convincing motive. His presence at the dinner the night of Ethan's death gives him the opportunity. And until you were kidnapped, it was starting to seem hopeless." Devon's shoulders dropped.

"And now?" Adele asked anxiously.

"Now, thanks to Desoto, we have a case for reasonable doubt."

Amelia shook her head. "But as I said, I'm sure Gabriel didn't do this."

Devon nodded, "And as I said, I agree with you, but that doesn't mean the prosecution needs to know we suspect that."

"But...is that legal?" Amelia looked around, making sure no one was within earshot.

"Legal? Yes. Ethical? I'm still working that out in my mind. But as Bennett's attorney, I'm obligated and permitted to do everything in my power to prove that there is doubt that he did this. And as much as we're all convinced Desoto didn't kill Ethan, we don't actually have evidence that he didn't."

Amelia looked at Adele for a second, waiting for her reaction. She could see the hope in her sister's eyes. They might be able to free the man she loved from his horrendous predicament that Amelia had placed him in from the start. Amelia knew what she had to do.

"I suppose you're right," she said, nodding to Devon.

Devon looked between the sisters and then reached out his hand to cover Amelia's where it sat on the table. "I promise, Amelia, you won't have to lie under oath. I'll be very careful with my questioning."

Looking down at his hand covering hers, Amelia shuddered as she remembered how relieved she had been the moment he'd burst into the cabin that morning. She looked up into his face and knew that shI don't think I've ever been so tirede trusted him.

"Okay," she said. "We can do this."

Relieved, Devon smiled. "Wonderful. I'm hoping your testimony will be brief. It will certainly be from my end, but I can't guarantee the prosecution won't adamantly push their case, regardless of what you've been through."

"I know you'll do your best, Devon." Amelia tried to smile, but she was already weary just thinking about the day to come.

Sensing her sister's exhaustion, Adele stood up and tugged gently on Amelia's arm. "Come on, Millie. We need to get you to bed."

Devon stood as well. "Of course. Let me escort you up to your room."

Amelia smiled up at him gratefully and nodded as they slowly climbed the stairs. Once she and Adele had entered their room, Adele secured the lock and turned around, inclining her body back against the door." I don't think I've ever been so tired. I can't imagine how you must be feeling. Let's get you out of those clothes and to bed."

She crossed to her trunk, pulled out Amelia's favorite nightgown, and handed it to her.

"Here, this was being cleaned when you left, and I just knew you'd rather have it than any of the ones you packed when we found you."

It was such a small gesture, but Amelia couldn't stop the tears that sprang to her eyes as she gripped the familiar fabric. Adele looked surprised and pulled her quickly into her arms.

"Oh, Millie. It's okay. It's all going to be okay." Stroking her sister's hair while she clung to her arms, Adele gently helped Amelia into the nightgown and then laid her down into the bed. Too exhausted to formulate words, Amelia nodded weakly in affirmation at her sister and closed her eyes. Adele extinguished the candle, careful not to awaken her sister who had already fallen into a deep sleep, safe once again.

The sun was high in the sky before Amelia dared to open her eyes the next morning. Peeking out of the comfort of the hotel bed sheets, she looked around for Adele and was at first alarmed to realize she was alone in the room. Panic seized her as she sat up, clenching her blanket around her chest protectively. Her eyes darted around the room. Sure she would see signs of a struggle, she became terrified, thinking that

Adele had also been taken. Why hadn't she heard her? Had they knocked her unconscious first? Her breath quickening, she flung off the covers and ran to her trunk to change into a dress. Not finding her petticoat, she began to fling clothes out of the trunk in frustration. "Where is it?" she screamed.

The door swung open. Amelia whipped around, ready to defend herself and saw Adele standing in the doorway, holding a small silver tray filled with food. Adele's eyes widened in alarm at the state of the room. "What on earth?"

"Adele!" Amelia yelped, running across the room to fling her arms around her sister.

"Amelia, what is it? What's wrong?"

"I thought they'd taken you!"

Quickly, Adele set the tray on the settee and cupped her sister's face in her hands. "Oh, dear, I'm fine. I was downstairs getting some breakfast for you, see? I brought up some blueberry pastries. Your favorite. Had I known you were so hungry you'd resort to destroying the room in my absence, I'd have asked them to throw on some eggs, too," she grinned and smiled comfortingly.

Ashamed, Amelia felt her cheeks grow warm. "Breakfast. Of course. Oh, I'm such a mess. I'm so sorry, Adele."

Shrugging it off, Adele laughed. "After what you've been through, Millie, I don't blame you one bit. But you'll have a heart attack if you react that way over every little thing. I left you a note on the desk, see?"

Crossing the room to the writing desk, Amelia saw her sister had indeed left a note detailing where she was going and what time they were expected at court.

"Devon managed to get your testimony delayed until after lunch, so we have the morning to relax."

Breathing a sigh of relief at this temporary reprieve, Amelia walked to the window and peered out through the dainty lace curtain that covered it. The day was as dreary as she felt. Rain drizzled lazily to the ground as she watched people painstakingly stepping over the puddles beginning to form on the walkways along the busy street. Turning back and crossing the room to her trunk, she pulled out a deep yellow poplar skirt and matching chemise. It was dreadfully wrinkled, but she suspected the men at court wouldn't mind, and she certainly didn't have time to send it to be pressed, so she put it on anyway. She topped it with a button-down black jersey blouse to keep her shielded from the rain.

Adele helped her pin back her hair into a loose chignon. Amelia nervously tugged at her hair, allowing messy curls to fall beside her ears. Smoothing her skirt, she pinned on a brown hat and followed her sister out the door and down into the lobby.

Once they were seated and served soup and tea, the girls sat eating in a tense silence until, finally, Amelia blurted out, "Gabriel Desoto thinks Father was involved with Ethan's murder."

The spoon in Amelia's hand clattered onto her saucer, and Adele dabbed at the splatter it created on her skirt. "That's absolutely ridiculous! Besides, why on earth would we consider anything that man has to say relevant?"

"Because Father gave Ethan most of the money he needed to initiate his railroad investment."

Adele's jaw dropped in shock. "How much?"

Shaking her head, Amelia replied, "I'm not sure. But Father admitted it to me himself right after the murder. He just didn't indicate how much. Desoto filled in that detail."

"How do we know Desoto was telling the truth?"

"The only thing Desoto cared about was how much money he lost and finding a way to get it back. Why would he lie about the amount?"

She sat for a moment, as if racking her brain, and then shook her head. "No reason that I can think of."

"Right. So, assuming Father did give Ethan most of the money he needed, that would have been ten thousand dollars at least. When the investment went sour, maybe they argued, and Father just overreacted."

"But even if Father did lose that much money, it's simply not in his character to do such a thing."

"Of course it isn't. Which is why I feel so hopelessly confused. I can't justify what I know to be my father as a man and how he may have acted from a business perspective. As much as he's been near to us as we've grown, we haven't seen him at work much at all. Maybe there he has a temper."

Amelia fell silent again, and Adele shook her head adamantly. "No. Millie. No. We're not going to do this again. This is how we ended up in this situation in the first place. How Bennett ended up here. I can't make myself believe that anyone I know had anything to do with this. If it wasn't Desoto, which, I agree with you after what you shared about your captivity, then it must have been a stranger."

"I want to believe that, Adele, I do. And please, trust me, I have no intention of sharing these thoughts with anyone but you. I just needed to tell *someone*. If Bennett is exonerated, and we all go home, then I'll look into Father's investment further before mentioning this to anyone else."

Adele's chin began to quiver, and she wiped a tear from the corner of her eye. "Please mean that, Amelia. I know that you're hurting. I know you miss Ethan, and I know you want to know who did this. We all do. But you've nearly ruined Bennett's life already."

Amelia started to object, but Adele held up her hand. "And I know you didn't mean for that to happen. But it did. And now he's on trial for the murder of his own brother because you couldn't keep your suspicions to yourself. So please, let's keep this between us. I *know* that Father did not kill Ethan. He wouldn't be capable of that if he lost a million dollars. He just didn't do it."

They ate in reserved silence for the remainder of the meal, each afraid to upset the other. The silence continued as they walked to the courthouse until, finally, they approached the first step, and Amelia suddenly felt her body seize up in a deep-rooted panic.

Adele turned from her perch on the third stair and looked back down at her.

"Millie, are you all right?"

Taking a few deep breaths, Amelia willed herself to take the first step. "I think so."

Adele nodded sympathetically. "I understand. Here, take my arm. I promise I won't leave your side."

Amelia did as her sister asked and the girls entered the building and found a seat outside the courtroom where Bennett's trial had been underway since before the breakfast hour. Amelia fingered one of the buttons on her jacket over and over for what seemed like hours until the door to the courtroom swung open, and she heard the bailiff call, "The court will now hear testimony from Miss Amelia Sullivan."

She felt Adele's hand grasp hers tightly and squeeze in encouragement as she took a deep breath and shakily stood to her feet. She made her way carefully past the counsel tables and up to the witness box.

Just breathe, Amelia.

She began to sit down in the chair but was startled when the judge cleared his throat and said, "You'll need to stand for the oath, if you please, Miss Sullivan."

Blushing, Amelia nodded quickly and straightened back up to her feet. "Of course. Please excuse me." Placing her hand on the Bible provided by the bailiff, Amelia swore to tell the truth to the best of her ability, so help her, God.

As he had with Nancy, Mr. Herringbone greeted Amelia and then proceeded right into the questioning.

"Miss Sullivan, you were engaged to be married to the deceased, Ethan Bennigan, am I correct?"

"Yes, sir."

"And how did you meet Mr. Bennigan?"

"We grew up together in Moon Springs. We played together when we were little." She tried to ignore the happy memories that had begun to flash through her mind.

"And when were you two engaged?"

"Last year."

"I see. And was that before or after Mr. Bennigan traveled to Savannah to meet with the railway investors?"

Realizing the niceties were over, Amelia answered, "Before, sir."

Mr. Herringbone turned and addressed the court, "Normally I would refer to the deceased by his last name out of respect, but as we are here for the trial of a man by the same last name, I will henceforth refer to the deceased by his given name, Ethan."

He turned back to face Amelia. "Miss Sullivan, you are also related to Ethan's sister, is that right?"

"Yes, sir. May is married to my brother. She's my sister-in-law."

"And you are also on friendly terms with the defendant, Mr. Bennett Bennigan?"

"Yes. He is one of my closest friends. As I said, we all grew up together."

"So, since you are familiar with all of the Bennigan siblings, I would anticipate that you may

196

have been privy to some of their business operations throughout the years."

"Not really, no."

Mr. Herringbone looked back towards the small audience and chuckled, which annoyed Amelia immensely. "You've never been at their office when they were conducting business? You've never met anyone else involved in their financial affairs? They've never taken you to see the result of a good investment?"

"I suppose, on occasion, but if you're asking if I was aware of the details of any of their partnerships, definitely not. I'm not officially tied to their business in any way, so it would have been completely unethical for them to divulge the details of their accounts to me."

"I see. They never, not once, discussed anything related to their business in your presence?"

Again, memories, this time of that last meal at her parents' table the night Ethan died. She hesitated —"I..."—and stopped. She looked desperately at Devon. He looked concerned but nodded for her to go ahead and tell the truth.

"Yes, I suppose they may have brought up their business when I was around occasionally. But not enough for me to know any particular details of any transactions."

"Ah! I see. So, you wouldn't be able to indicate whether or not they ever had any disagreements over any of Ethan's recent business decisions? Say, involving the railroad from Savannah he had invested in?"

197

Amelia's shoulders slumped as she realized she couldn't answer this question in generalities. She looked at Bennett, trying as hard as she could to apologize without speaking. He dropped his eyes and turned away. She looked back at the attorney and cleared her throat.

"Yes. Yes, I did hear them discussing the railroad deal before Ethan died."

Mr. Herringbone smiled. "And was that a peaceful conversation?"

Ethan's protests, which had boomed from behind the closed door in her family's house, were so loud in Amelia's head, it was as if he was there in the courtroom, yelling at his brother.

"No, sir. It was not."

"And in this tense conversation between the Bennigan brothers did the defendant, Bennett Bennigan, blame Ethan for the poor financial state their business was in following the collapse of the railroad deal?"

Amelia frowned, frustrated that she had to say anything negative about Bennett, but then sensed a small opportunity to perhaps turn the tide in his favor.

"No," she insisted. "I wouldn't say he blamed him. It was more that he was concerned that Ethan was planning to continue pursuing the railroad after it went wrong the first time."

"Interesting. Could you elaborate please? Was there another deal Ethan was considering? Something that Bennett did not approve of?"

She knew this moment was critical, and she had to tread carefully. "Ethan had been considering

198

investing more money in the railroad group still hoping to bring one to Oak County. But Bennett didn't trust the man who would be the primary investor in that deal."

"And who was that?"

"Gabriel Desoto."

Mr. Herringbone inhaled a shocked breath as murmurs erupted in the crowd at the mention of Desoto's name. She noted that even the jurors seemed taken aback. She relaxed ever so slightly, grateful that her gamble had paid off. Now she just needed to plant enough doubt in their minds without having to admit that she believed Gabriel was actually innocent of the murder.

Frantically shuffling the papers on the prosecution table, Mr. Herringbone looked up at her and regained his composure.

"Gabriel Desoto. Yes, I've heard of him. I understand he has an unscrupulous reputation for shrewd business maneuvers, but the county was not informed that there was a connection between him and this case. Are you certain Ethan and Bennett were arguing about Gabriel Desoto?"

Amelia nodded emphatically. "Absolutely. Mr. Desoto spent several weeks after Ethan's murder in town, trying to recoup some of the money he'd lost in the deal."

"How do you know that is why Mr. Desoto was in town?"

"Because he told me."

Laughter rippled through the crowd, which was mostly composed of men. Amelia could feel her anger mounting in spite of herself.

Mr. Herringbone also chuckled dismissively. "Now, pardon me, Miss Sullivan, but are you expecting us to believe that Gabriel Desoto, a seasoned businessman, approached you about regaining funds from your dead fiancé? That doesn't sound very gentlemanly." He turned his face to the members of the crowd as if they, too, were in on the joke.

Amelia didn't falter. "I have discovered through personal experience that Gabriel Desoto knows nothing about manners. Yes, he did approach me about the money he claimed he'd lost with Ethan. He was very determined to get it back."

"Personal experience? You have a relationship with Mr. Desoto?"

"Not by choice."

"And what is the nature of your relationship?"

"Well, he took it upon himself to fraternize with my family after Ethan's death, no doubt trying to determine how to get his hands on the money."

"So you saw him socially?"

"On a few occasions, yes."

"Romantically?"

Amelia wanted to jump over the table and slap Herringbone in the face, but refrained. Instead she muttered, "Please, sir, don't insult me."

Holding up his hands, the lawyer replied, "No insult intended, Miss Sullivan. I'm just trying to wrap my head around why you would know anything about Mr. Desoto's business. That is, unless you're merely being inventive in order to detract our attention from the defendant?"

His eyes challenged hers. Amelia hesitated. Her plan had been foiled much sooner than she'd hoped. She knew this wouldn't be enough of a distraction of suspicion from Bennett to be effective. But she also knew she couldn't lie and suddenly accuse Desoto of the murder. She looked at Devon for help, but she could tell he had none to give.

A cough cut through the tense silence of the room. Amelia glanced around the court to see her sister tapping her chest as if to silence a cough, but she looked intently at Amelia and nodded. Amelia knew Adele was giving her permission to tell the truth.

Looking up at Mr. Herringbone, Amelia answered evenly, "Actually, Mr. Desoto courted my younger sister, Adele, for a short time following Ethan's death. That's how I was privy to many conversations with him."

Herringbone's eyebrows rose amusingly. "Your sister? I see."

She could see he was struggling with how to respond favorably to his case against Bennett, so Amelia seized the opportunity to continue. "Yes, she spent time with him for several weeks. Anyone can confirm that. He attended family dinners, parties, and several other occasions. We also attended a picnic at the farm he owns in the county. So, you see, I had plenty of opportunity to get to know him, as he did me, and he used those instances to press me for ways he could regain the money he'd lost through Ethan. And, as I said, he was persistent."

"And your sister, is she still courting Mr. Desoto?"

"No, thankfully, she is not."

"So he got his money back then?"

Triumph rallied through Amelia's body. This was the question she'd been hoping for, the one she knew she could answer honestly that would fully expose the character, or lack thereof, of Gabriel Desoto which might be enough to exonerate Bennett without the need to falsely implicate Desoto. "Well, he hadn't when he kidnapped me two days ago, and now he is sitting in the county prison, so I suspect not."

Herringbone whipped around to stare at Amelia, slack-jawed. The judge, who had remained silent throughout the testimony, looked down at her in alarm. "Miss Sullivan, can you repeat that, please?"

"Gabriel Desoto had me kidnapped from this courthouse two days ago in an attempt to regain his lost funds and to stop me from bringing up his name in court."

At that instant, Amelia knew she'd won. If Herringbone trod further down the road of asking her why Desoto wouldn't want her testifying in court, it would only hurt his case. Even though she knew she wasn't going to accuse Gabriel of murder under oath, Herringbone didn't. He was stuck.

There was a moment of painful silence as she saw Herringbone consider the situation before he emitted a sincere smile and said quietly, "Miss Sullivan, I am afraid that is the worst thing I've heard in all of my years as a prosecutor. I'm mighty glad to see you are unharmed and to hear that Mr. Desoto has been apprehended." Looking up at the judge, he declared, "The county has no further questions for Miss Sullivan."

The judge nodded and looked at Devon. "Would the defense like to question the witness?"

Devon stood and shook his head. "No, your honor. We have no questions for Miss Sullivan, although the entire defensive team, and Mr. Bennigan, are certainly glad Miss Sullivan has been recovered safely from her wretched ordeal at the hands of an evil criminal."

Amelia couldn't suppress the half smile that appeared on her face as she silently thanked Devon for doing his part to shift the blame without perjuring himself.

The judge nodded. "The court agrees. Miss Sullivan, you may step down, and if I may give some personal advice, please, take care of yourself."

She smiled gratefully as she stood to return to her seat. "Thank you, Your Honor. I will certainly do that."

The judge looked over to the box and addressed the jury. "The court will recess for the day. We will reconvene first thing tomorrow."

Everyone stood to exit, and Amelia reached over the gallery bench to hug Adele who hurried up to her. "I'm so sorry you had to be dragged back into this mess."

Adele squeezed her back reassuringly. "No, Millie, it's fine. I'm so glad it worked!"

"Me, too."

The sisters quickly exited the courthouse and returned to their hotel to have some hot tea and pastries and wait for Devon. The change in the emotional atmosphere was astounding for both of them. What was once nervousness and apprehension had been replaced by hope and anticipation. Amelia knew she'd done all she could to help free Bennett, and now all she could do was pray that it had been enough.

That evening, they took their previous table next to the fireplace which had now been kindled to combat the chilly air and sipped quietly on chamomile tea. Although the chaos of the past few days had left her tired and longing for bed, Amelia willed herself to stay so that she could glean Devon's insight into the day's events. She was pleasantly surprised when she saw him bounding into the hotel less than an hour after court had adjourned. She'd expected him to stay late with Bennett, strategizing for his testimony the next day.

When he saw them sitting at the table, his smile nearly consumed his face. He hurried to join them and sat down. Amelia started to ask him about her testimony, but he put up his hand to interrupt her. "You did beyond well, Millie. They're letting him out!" Amelia was confused. She looked at Adele for explanation but could find none on the face of her equally bewildered sister.

"Devon, I don't understand. What do you mean, let him out?"

"Herringbone knew you brought enough doubt to Bennett's guilt by bringing up Desoto that the jury might exonerate him, and then he'd also have to try Desoto. He doesn't have the courage to indict Gabriel Desoto for murder. He's too powerful and has too many friends. So, the county dropped the charges against Bennett! He'll be released in the morning as soon as the judge signs off on the case."

Adele burst into tears, and Amelia rushed around the table to take her in her arms while, at the same time, grabbing Devon's hand. "Thank you, Devon. For everything," she said.

He squeezed her hand back warmly."Of course. He's family." Devon paused, his voice wavering. "You're all family."

They stayed downstairs, chatting about the details and processes involved in getting Bennett released from custody, then Adele excused herself for bed—the events of the past few days finally catching up with her. The relief of such good news after months of turmoil had the opposite effect on Amelia, who suddenly had a great boost of unexpected energy and decided to stay downstairs.

Devon escorted Adele to her room and dropped off his files in his own while Amelia ordered them both another cup of tea from the kitchen and sat on the loveseat closest to the fireplace. She hoped the chamomile would settle her down enough so that she could eventually sleep in spite of the anticipation of Bennett's release, so she sipped eagerly when it arrived.

Chamomile had always been Ethan's favorite tea as well. May used to tease him for drinking something so floral when most other men preferred a strong black tea with, maybe, a touch of lemon. But he was always insistent it was the best.

"Civilizations have been using tea for centuries for its medicinal properties—not because it tastes good. I happen to think chamomile fulfills both of those requirements. The way I see it, the earthier the flavor, the more of the earth's benefits you're getting. Nothing says 'earthy' like a drink that tastes like leaves," Ethan always said.

Amelia giggled audibly.

"What's so funny?" Devon asked.

Amelia startled as she snapped back to the present. "Pardon?"

Sitting down next to her, Devon nodded to her cup.

"You were laughing at your tea."

"Was I?" She leaned over and picked up his cup and saucer and handed it to him. "I was just thinking about Ethan."

"Ah. Chamomile, yes?"

This time she chortled loudly. "Yes. He shared his theories with you, too, I suppose?"

"Mmhmm," he affirmed, taking a slow sip of his tea. "I see the merits of his argument, but I'm much obliged that you got me plain black because I prefer my tea to taste like tea, not dirt."

"Noted."

They both fell silent for a while, lost in memories. After a bit, Amelia tilted her head and looked up at Devon. His face was sad, but his eyes still held their usual kindness and intensity.

"You remind me of him, you know."

"Do I?"

"Yes. There's the obvious familial resemblance, of course. But you're so similar in other ways, too.

Your work ethic, your determination, your passion for what you believe in."

Surprising herself with her openness, Amelia ducked her head and reached up to see if her cheeks were as hot as they felt. They were.

Devon must have sensed her discomfort because he quickly spoke.

"Thank you, Amelia. But you're wrong."

Puzzled, she looked up at him.

"Really, you should say he reminds you of me. I'm older."

Grateful for his merciful lightening of the mood, she laughed. "I suppose that's fair."

She took another sip, then put her cup down on the saucer and sighed.

"You look tired. Can I escort you to your room?"

"I'm settling down, I think, but I do still feel restless. I know I should be so relieved the trial is over, and I am, especially for Bennett's sake. But in another way, I feel like nothing was really accomplished even after all of this. Part of me feels like we're further away than we were before from finding any answers. Bennett didn't kill Ethan. But now I'm almost sure that Gabriel didn't either. So where does that leave us?"

Devon put his hand on her face and turned it to look at his.

"It leaves you back home in your own bed where you're safe. And that's what matters the most to me. You have no idea how scared I was when you disappeared, Amelia. I didn't know how I was going to find you, and unlike Ethan's murder, I knew who had done it. But that made it worse because I knew what Desoto was capable of. If they had done you more harm than they did…if any of them had…"

He stopped, trying to choke back his emotions, but Amelia saw his eyes glistening and felt her own following suit.

She wrapped her hands around his, which were now both holding her face.

"But they didn't. I'm sore, but I'll heal. And it wasn't your fault Devon."

"I should have—"

"—Devon. It *wasn't* your fault."

Closing his eyes, he leaned his forehead against hers and sighed, his breath warm and sweet on her face.

Chapter 13

Bennett's release from prison was welcomingly uneventful, and the foursome headed home late the next morning. The carriage lurched away from the courthouse, and while the other three travelers casually conversed about the lack of humidity for an August morning, Amelia simply stared out the window in silence.

Bennett sensed her unease and leaned over to speak to her softly. "Millie, thank you for what you did to help get me released."

She started to protest, but he held his hand up and continued. "Please, don't apologize for the rest of it. Ethan was murdered. You were his fiancée, and everything the county said about me was true. It made sense that I was arrested. I would have done the same thing."

"But you lost months of your life, your reputation, and you never even got a chance to grieve for your brother in private."

Tears shone in the corners of his eyes. "Yes. That's all true. But none of that was your fault. You were just searching for answers, like we all were. If it hadn't have been you, someone else would have come to the same conclusion eventually. The best thing we can do now is mend our bond and move forward. I don't have to tell you that it's what Ethan would have wanted."

Tears were now streaming down Amelia's cheeks, and she nodded. "You're right."

Bennett sat back and leaned against the carriage back stay. "Then we won't discuss it again."

They had no sooner turned down the path leading up to the house when the front door burst open and May ran down the stairs, holding baby Ethan in her arms. Regardless of the mixture of emotions in the cabin among the four companions, there was only pure joy emanating from May's face when they rolled up to the front of the Bennigan house an hour later.

She waved frantically as they pulled up to the house, rushed the carriage to open the door, and practically pulled Bennett from his seat. "You're home! I can't believe this is really over!" she cried, clinging to her brother's neck with her free arm.

"I am certainly delighted to see you, too, May, but I must admit my sole focus is on meeting this young gentleman here before me." He scooped the baby from her arms and kissed his cherubic red cheeks. "Hello there, little Ethan. I'm Uncle Bennett. We're going to be great friends. I'm going to teach you to eat well, laugh often, and perhaps study the art of carpentry, because I've heard your father lacks the necessary skills in that area."

Everyone laughed and climbed the stairs to the house where they were greeted by the rest of the Sullivan family. When the telegram had arrived that morning announcing Bennett's release from prison, Mrs. Sullivan had thrown together a welcoming luncheon in a whirl and the family traveled to be there together to welcome Bennett.

As they walked into the dining room, Juliette threw up her hands in exasperation and exclaimed, "Oh, and Bennett, I *must* apologize. The baker said he simply couldn't whip together a cake at such short notice, so you'll just have to settle for the éclairs he'd already made first thing this morning."

Bennett erupted into laughter.

"What is it, dear? Do you not like éclairs?" Juliette asked, surprised.

"Mrs. Sullivan, I haven't had anything in my mouth with even a pinch of sweetness in it for months. You could shove a spoonful of sugar down my throat, and I'd still sing your praises. Éclairs will be heavenly. Thank you."

They spent a relaxing afternoon filling Bennett in on all of the town's happenings and letting him get more acquainted with the baby before Adele stood and said, "I do think we should all leave and let Bennett get some rest now. I'm sure you're exhausted," she said to him.

He smiled affectionately at Adele, a smile which was not lost on Amelia, as he agreed, "Yes. I suppose I would like to sleep in a real bed for a change. Thank you all for such a warm welcome home at such short notice. I'll be sure to drop by in the morning so we can continue my reintroduction to society." He turned to Devon. "You have been staying here, haven't you? I'm not used to sleeping alone anymore. I'd like you to stay, at least for tonight."

Devon smiled. "I have indeed been staying here, but in your room. I'll just run up and move my things to the guest room. It won't take me but a moment."

May chimed in. "Devon, why don't you move into Ethan's room? It's much larger and has a much better view, and it's not like he'll be needing it anytime soon." She stopped suddenly and held her hand up to her mouth. "Oh, I'm sorry. That sounded so insensitive."

Crossing the room to put his arms around his sister, Bennett assured her, "No, you're right, he won't need it." He looked around the room and announced firmly, "If there's one positive thing I gained from my months in prison, it was time to come to terms with the fact that my brother is gone, and he's not coming back, and that he wouldn't want us to continue milling around half expecting him to return. We need to move on." Turning back to Devon, Bennett nodded towards the stairs. "May is right. That room is much nicer than the guest room. And it's yours now, for however long you stay and whenever you come back to visit."

He called to their one and only servant. "Eliza, please kindly move Devon's things from my room into the room across the hall. It will be his permanently."

Eliza's eyebrows rose slightly, but she said nothing and proceeded up the stairs. Devon bid everyone else farewell and followed her to assist in moving his things.

Amelia shooed everyone towards the front hall. As they opened the door to exit, Bennett shyly cleared his throat and indicated to Adele he'd like to speak with her for a moment.

Desperate to stay and hear what he had to say to her sister, Amelia was annoyed when her mother nudged her out the door with a knowing look. The rest of her family climbed into the carriages that would take them home, but Amelia pretended to lose her shoe and stopped outside on the front stoop until her sister emerged a moment later, her face rosy with excitement.

Bennett nodded at both of them. "Good afternoon, Millie, Adele. I'll see you all tomorrow. Thank you again."

"Goodbye, Bennett." Amelia smiled as the door closed behind him and turned to Adele expectantly.

Adele grabbed her arm and pulled her towards the carriage.

"Not now, Millie," she whispered anxiously. "I know I'll not be able to hear the end of it from Mother. I'll tell you what he said once we're home."

Grimacing with frustration, Amelia climbed into the carriage and rode home to Sullivan's Pine with May and her brother and the baby, while Adele rode with their parents. But as soon as they ascended the stairs to their room, Amelia yanked her sister inside and set her on the bed in front of her.

"All right, now, you exasperating child. What did he say to you?"

Looking down shyly, Adele played with the hem on her skirt and said quietly, "I'm not one to give you the full details of such a personal conversation, but in summary, he said that he'd wasted too much of his life planning for a certain future, and Ethan's death made him realize that he needed to live presently, because the future isn't promised to anyone." She paused, looking up to ensure she wasn't upsetting her sister.

Not satisfied, Amelia pressed her further. "Of course, Ethan's death has done that for everyone. He could have said that in front of a hundred people. What else did he say? What did he say that he wanted only *you* to hear?"

Ducking her head away, Adele whispered, "He said I am his present…and his future."

Amelia nearly toppled her sister in excitement.

"Oh Adele! He proposed to you? Right there at the front door?"

Adele looked up, confused. "Well, I don't know. Was that a proposal?"

"It's as close to one without it being one, I'd say. He probably wants to discuss it with Father first, and he hasn't had an opportunity to do that yet, obviously, but, oh Adele! I think this is it! He loves you! I knew he did! Oh, I'm so happy for you!" Amelia hugged her sister again.

"Thank you," Adele said, her smile infectious. "I still can't really believe it myself. I honestly didn't think he'd ever get out of prison. It never crossed my mind that we could ever have a future together."

"Well, you do. A long, beautiful future. I'm going to make sure of it!"

Adele folded her arms. "How are *you* going to make sure of anything?"

Getting up from the bed, Amelia crossed the room and pulled out the keepsake box full of wedding gown sketches, swatches of fabric and paper samples she'd used when planning her wedding to Ethan.

"We're going to start by making sure you're the most beautiful bride Oak County has ever seen."

They spent the rest of the evening pouring over everything. By bedtime, Adele had decided that, in contrast to Amelia's desire for a small, simple ceremony, she wanted a large wedding followed by a dance in the ballroom of their home. They pledged not to mention a word of their plans in the vicinity of their mother until Bennett had talked with their father, as he would likely scold them for planning a wedding for a girl who wasn't officially engaged yet, no matter how eager she was to plan such an affair.

The next afternoon, Adele and Amelia were in the courtyard that ran along the side of the house when they heard the crunching of hooves on the gravel of the main drive. Adele's eyes gleamed with excited anticipation as she peeked around the corner of the house and turned back to indicate that it was indeed Devon and Bennett arriving at Sullivan's Pine and that her father had greeted them at the door and had invited Bennett inside. Devon returned to the carriage to pull it around to the stable.

Amelia stepped forward quickly to pull Adele back into the garden. "Now, don't let him see you," she instructed her sister. "He's probably so nervous already, the poor thing. One look at you and he might lose his nerve, and you'll have to wait another who knows how long for a formal proposal."

"Oh, but I can't just sit here twiddling with flowers. I need something to entertain me, or I'll lose my mind."

"Who is losing her mind?" Devon inquired as he walked around the corner.

"Adele," Amelia stated matter-of-factly. "She's simply beside herself with anticipation of Bennett asking my father's permission to marry her, and she needs something to distract her."

"Now, who said anything about Bennett asking Mr. Sullivan for your hand, Adele?" he teased. "I've heard nothing of the sort."

Amelia swatted at him. "Oh, stop it. He talked to her about it yesterday. Don't send her into a tizzy."

Devon guffawed. "He's already asked you? How ungentlemanly and anti-climactic that makes the whole thing."

Ignoring him, Adele tried to peek into the library through the window, but Amelia grabbed her arm. "Adele, I'm serious. You'll frighten him to death. Let the poor man do what he came to do."

Adele sighed in exasperation and collapsed dramatically onto a bench. Then she looked up at her sister and friend. "Well then, someone say something to keep my mind off the two men holding my future in their hands behind those walls."

Amelia smirked. "Oh, don't get me started on that. You hold your own future in your hands. You could marry that silly, no-brained stock boy at the mercantile if you want to. This is just a frivolous formality."

"Well said, Amelia." Devon applauded as he affectionately patted Adele's shoulder. "It's just a silly tradition. Honestly, after the year he's had, your father could laugh in his face, and I think Bennett would

216

whisk you away and marry you anyway. You have nothing to worry about."

Amelia nodded. "But all the same, Devon, please do something to distract us both. I'm not one for dramatic tension."

Devon reached into his satchel and pulled out a small ledger book. "Well, I do have this. I'm not sure how you feel about continuing to pursue Ethan's killer, Millie, and I will completely understand if you want to leave it to the authorities." He paused, waiting for Amelia to confirm or deny his sentiment.

She snatched the book out of his hand. "What is this? I don't recall seeing this book when you and I went through Ethan's office."

"That's because it wasn't in his office. It was in the desk in his bedroom at the house. It seems, at first glance, to be a duplicate ledger copy of the transactions from the business for the past two years. But something didn't seem quite right, so I went to the office this morning and pulled out the other one, and I was right on both accounts. It is practically identical, except for one thing."

He had opened both books on the garden table and pointed to a section in each with his fingers. It only took Amelia half a second to recognize the difference. She looked up at Devon.

"I don't understand. Why would the amount he borrowed from Gabriel Desoto be *less* in the ledger he hid in his room? If anything, I would think he would do the opposite."

"Exactly. In fact, this one I found last night indicates that he borrowed less than half the amount the office records indicate he did."

"Well, we know how much he was indebted to the investors for overall," Amelia said as she flipped to the last page of the ledger scored with Ethan's calculations and confirmed that the amounts Ethan owed in total were the same. "So, where did the rest of the money come from?"

"Here." Devon turned a few pages back from the Desoto transaction and indicated an area of the ledger that had been furiously scribbled out. "This is the only other portion of the books that differ. The discrepancy has to be here."

"But you can't make it out." Amelia frowned, holding it up to the sunlight at different angles with the same result.

"I've tried that. I've tried candlelight, firelight, every kind of light."

"How frustrating," Amelia growled. "The answer to everything could be right here, and we just can't read it."

Adele took the book from Amelia's hands and turned the page over, gently rubbing her fingers along the backside.

She looked back up at them. "Have you tried rubbing it?"

"Pardon?" Devon laughed. "Like you're doing? Is there some sort of mystical power in your fingers that transfers through the page into your mind?"

Adele wasn't amused. "No. I meant have you tried rubbing something over the indentations with something to transfer the marks to another paper."

Amelia's pulse quickened. She grabbed the book and began sprinting towards the back door of the house. "Adele!" she called over her shoulder. "That's brilliant!"

It took Amelia no more than a minute to grab some charcoal and paper from her mother's art supplies, and she hurried back out to the garden. Devon still looked confused, so Adele explained as Amelia began the tedious task. "Mother taught us how to make leaf rubbings with charcoal when we were younger. You put the leaf under the paper and then rub on top of it, and the bumps from the veins of the leaf come through the paper, leaving an outline. If you do it very lightly, it may work the same way with the indentations from the pen on the ledger paper."

Ever so carefully, Amelia laid a fresh piece of paper atop the marred page and barely brushed the area with the charcoal. It took a few seconds, but the result was exactly as they'd hoped, albeit in reverse.

"Now who can figure out what this says since it's upside down?" Amelia asked, looking up at them.

Examining her rubbing, Devon began copying the image, one letter and number at a time, onto a blank page of the other ledger. After several excruciating minutes, they had a better picture of what lay beneath the scribbles.

Adele read out loud, "July, 1892 – one thousand, four hundred dollars to S.R. – M.S. August,

1892 – two thousand, two hundred dollars to S.R. – PdS"

The sisters looked up at Devon. His face was grim.

"S.R. is how he labels Savannah Railroad in his accounts. So M.S. must be…" He hesitated.

"Michael Sullivan," Amelia finished for him. She turned to Adele and spoke barely above a whisper, "That's an awful lot of money, Adele."

Adele nodded solemnly. "But that doesn't necessarily mean—"

"—It might," Amelia interrupted. "We have to face that possibility."

She knew Devon thought the same but was too compassionate to verbalize his agreement. He frowned again, looking at the book. "I don't know who PdS is, though. And they sank more money into the railroad than your father did. We can't jump to any conclusions until we confirm that man's identity."

Sitting back in exasperation, Amelia frowned. "Even if we knew the identity of PdS, it doesn't explain why Ethan would have attributed more capital to Desoto than he had actually put in. Why tie yourself more tightly to such a nefarious character?"

"Well, if M.S. really is your father, and he was trying to keep his investment off the official books, PdS must have insisted on the same terms. He wanted to make sure no one going through the office records would know the identity of the real investors," Devon surmised.

"Ethan was trying to protect the investors, not himself," Adele concluded.

Amelia looked, with terrible longing, in the direction of the creek where he had fallen and said quietly, "Well I hope those people were worth protecting, because it likely got him killed," she cleared her throat. "We need to figure out who PdS is."

"You could ask your father if he knows," Devon suggested.

Gasping, Adele shook her head. "Oh no. We can't do that. We need to leave our father out of this!"

Amelia disagreed. "No, Adele, Devon is right. We do need to ask father about this. He might know who PdS is, and he might be able to shed light on the reason why Ethan covered up his investment in the first place." Adele looked unsure, but she said nothing more.

Presently Bennett emerged from the house and poked his head around the corner, calling to Devon, "I'm ready, Cousin. We'd best get a move on before it gets too late to get any work done clearing out Ethan's room."

He made eye contact with Adele, and his face flushed scarlet, but he said nothing to her directly. Amelia delighted in his shyness and bid them both farewell.

The rest of the afternoon did not present an opportunity for Amelia to speak privately with her father about the conflicting ledgers. The next morning, before the sun had fully risen, she climbed out of her bed and wrapped her lightweight pink cotton bathrobe over her shoulders and tiptoed down the stairs so as not to disturb the others in the house.

As she suspected, her father was already hard at work in his study, studying the summer season's

221

Burpee Seed Exchange Catalog and furiously scribbling out the week's sales order to be sent to Atlanta. As harvest season was only a few months away, he needed to begin stockpiling the mercantile warehouse with the latest farm equipment. Amelia watched him in silence for a moment and considered turning around and retreating to her room. She feared what the questions she had to ask him could do to their relationship if the conversation went awry. However, before she could make up her mind, he sensed her presence in the room and looked up to greet her with a smile.

"Well, good morning to you, early bird! I can't recall the last time I've seen you up and about at this dreadful hour," he said, the remnants of his ancestral Irish accent peeking through.

She crossed the room and seated herself opposite him at the desk. Deciding that the best way to bring up such a difficult topic was to come right out with it, Amelia began. "Father...I need to ask you some..." She paused, trying to come up with the right word—"unpleasant questions about..." A frown settled on her father's face as he nodded for her to continue. She tried to be brave and look him in the eye as she was taught, but her fear overcame her, and she looked down at the floor before concluding breathlessly, "Ethan's business affairs."

Michael cleared his throat and moved to stop her. "Amelia, we've been over this. It's just not your place to be asking questions about Ethan's business or mine. As much as you don't like it, it's a man's world, and there are so many other things..."

222

"Father," she interrupted, "Ethan had two separate ledgers listing his investors in the railroad. In one of them, the one he kept hidden, the amount invested by a man he recorded as M.S. was double the amount as was attributed to someone of the same initials in the ledger he kept in his office." She blurted this out so quickly, stumbling over the words, but she had to get them out before he interrupted her again. She looked up at her father and met his gaze. "Are you M.S.?"

Seeing no way out, he quietly responded, "Yes, I am."

"And did you invest twice as much as we knew about in the railroad?"

"Yes, I did."

"Did you lose it all when the railroad didn't come?"

"Yes, I did."

"Does Mother know?"

"No, she doesn't."

"Is the mercantile in trouble because of the bad investment?"

He hesitated, then replied, "Yes."

"Did you kill Ethan because of it?"

This time, there was no hesitation, and her father looked at her with a more sincere expression than any she had ever seen as he answered emphatically, "No, Amelia. I didn't kill Ethan. I didn't touch him. I don't care how much trouble we're in, that boy was like a son to me. I wouldn't hurt any man over money, but especially not Ethan." His tone had changed, and she noticed a tear brimming in his eye, threatening to escape down his cheek.

Amelia sat in silence for several moments and considered his answers. She considered the man she had known, loved, and grown up with, whose knee she had climbed on as a child—the man whom she had only ever known to be gentle, wise, and stable. The man who, even now, as she had nearly accused him of murder, didn't press her to drop the subject. He sat patiently waiting for her to process the interrogation she had just completed. Finally, Amelia leaned across the desk and grasped his hand, which she could see was trembling—out of anger, frustration or fear, she didn't know and didn't care. She looked into his face and nodded solemnly. "I believe you, Papa."

His face slackened in relief. "Thank you, Millie. I know you want answers. We all do. We just have to face the fact that we may never know who killed Ethan."

Amelia vehemently disagreed. "No, I feel the answers truly do lie in the differing ledgers. I just have to figure out which person lost enough in the investment to want him dead."

She stood to leave, then paused and turned back around. "Do you know someone with the initials PdS? Maybe a business elsewhere in the county?"

Michael thought for a moment and then shrugged his shoulders. "No one that I can think of, but if you really think the answers are in those books, keep looking, keep asking questions, and you'll figure it out. If anyone can do it, it's you."

She smiled at his confidence in her as she returned to her room and dressed quickly. She wanted to get to Ethan's office as soon as it was socially acceptable to be out and about in the morning. After a quick breakfast of toast and jam, she peered outside, noting that the weather was significantly warmer than it had been the day before. Seeing no clouds in the sky, she set off towards town on foot. She arrived at the Bennigan house at eight o'clock and knocked on the door. Bennett answered the door himself, a wet towel in his hand.

"Amelia, what in heaven's name are you doing out at this hour?"

She smirked at the shaving cream residue that covered his neck, grabbed the towel out of his hand, quickly wiped it off and stepped inside.

Bennett chuckled. "By all means, please do come in."

"Where is Devon?"

"I think he's out back, picking some peaches from the grove for breakfast."

"Perfect. I love your peaches."

She continued through the house and out onto the back terrace, down the stone steps and out into the garden. The aroma of the ripening peaches was intoxicating, and she paused for a moment to take it in. Scanned the immense grove for Devon, she spotted him just a bit ahead of her towards the southern boundary of the trees. He waved her over from his perch on a ladder where he was reaching high up into a particularly full tree.

"Good morning!" she said cheerfully as she approached.

"Good morning to you," Devon replied as he tossed a peach in her direction. "I've heard you're fond of these beauties."

Taking an eager bite, she nodded.

"You heard correctly. They're my favorite."

"I agree. They're like Heaven's nectar this time of year," he said as he climbed off the ladder and took a bite of his own. "Now please do tell me why I get the pleasure of your entrancing company so early this morning? I know you're not just here for the produce."

Amelia felt a wash of heat rise to her face briefly, but she ignored her sudden shyness and recounted her conversation with her father that morning as well as her intention to look through Ethan's books at the office for the identity of "PdS."

Devon was pensive for a moment, his eyes trained on the ground. Then he said, "Well, if we believe your father is telling the truth, and I do, then I agree that only thing left to do is determine the identity of PdS."

Looking into the half-full basket of peaches, Amelia climbed up on the ladder herself. "Well, I think we should be sure not to deprive the rest of the house of their peaches. Let's fill the basket first."

Devon reached up into the adjacent tree and obliged. Within minutes the basket was overflowing with fruit, and they passed through the kitchen on their way to the front stoop of the house. Bennett was still in the front room reading a book when they paused to say goodbye and share their intentions.

"You're welcome to come with us, Bennett," Devon said.

"Thank you, but I've got something else to take care of this morning," he said nervously, stepping from one foot to the other like a fidgety horse.

Amelia looked at Devon to see if he would reveal anything, but he only nodded and walked towards the door. She followed without comment, but as soon as they were outside she poked him in the ribs and whispered theatrically, "He's going to propose to my sister today, isn't he?"

"I've no idea."

She poked him again.

"Ouch! Was that really necessary? I know nothing," he claimed, although his eyes were twinkling.

The walk to town was a hot, but pleasant, one. Devon told Amelia about his law offices in Savannah. His partners had been corresponding with him over the past several weeks during his absence about their intentions to start a new office in either Atlanta or Charleston, and they wanted him to be the lead attorney at the new location.

"That's wonderful!" she said, but inside she felt pangs of disappointment.

"Thank you. It's certainly an honor, but I feel so out of touch with everything relating to my business since being here. I feel as if I'm not able to clearly lay out the advantages and disadvantages of each place."

Amelia considered both places in her mind. "Well, Charleston is a beautiful city, much like Savannah, but it's also a seaside city, so there's a limit to where you could expand from there aside from due

227

west. Atlanta puts you in a better position to make contacts to cities toward the west—more of an opportunity to grow later on down the road."

Devon laughed as they arrived at the office. "You see? I hadn't thought about it in that way. It's too bad I can't take you with me wherever I decide to go."

Blushing again, Amelia put the key in the door and pushed it open. They crossed the room to the desk where the ledgers were kept, pulled out each one from the past several years, and laid them on the desk. Devon yanked the one Ethan had been kept at the house from his satchel, and they spent the next hour going through each one, line by line, trying to find any hints as to the identity of the mystery investor. But each ledger led nowhere.

By lunchtime, Amelia's eyes were tired, and her neck was sore from bending over. She sat back in disgust. "This hasn't helped at all."

Devon disagreed. "That's not necessarily true. Now we know where not to look."

She sighed. "I suppose so, but I'm running out of ideas as to where to search."

"Me, too." Devon looked out the window for a moment and then back at Amelia. "Millie," he began slowly, "it might just be time to let this go."

Crossing her arms in protest, Amelia frowned. "I just can't bring myself to admit we might never know what happened to Ethan. It just seems so... unfair."

Devon leaned forward in his chair and gently slid her hand into his.

"Amelia, letting go of Ethan's murder doesn't mean letting go of Ethan."

She looked into his eyes. She hadn't considered this. But she knew he was right. Tears slid down her cheeks, and she looked around desperately for something to wipe them away with. But before she could find something, Devon was on the floor on both knees, pulling her into his arms. He held her like that for several minutes, wrapping her in a protective embrace, and she felt nothing but a strong sense of safety and empathy as she clung to his sleeves and wept. When she finally regained enough composure to sit back up, she couldn't find the words to thank him for seeing her through such a raw, personal moment, so she said nothing. He gently wiped away the remaining tears from her cheeks and stood up, helping her do the same.

Their walk back to her house was almost entirely silent, but it was peaceful. Devon intended to escort her home and return to the Bennigan house, but as they approached the front door, it swung open and Adele ran out and down the steps.

"Millie! You're here! I couldn't stand waiting another minute to tell you! Bennett proposed! We're getting married!"

The joy on her sister's face was palpable, and the emotional exhaustion of the morning melted away as Amelia celebrated with her. Bennett emerged from the house with a slightly embarrassed grin on his face, and Devon hopped up the steps to congratulate him.

"When is the wedding?" he asked.

"September first. We need a few weeks to get the food ordered, invitations out, and the dress altered, but we don't want to wait any longer than we have to."

Amelia was confused. "What dress?"

"Mother's! Waiting for a new one would take so long, I decided to have hers altered and to add a few strands of pearls along the hem from my collection."

Amused by her sister's sudden abandonment of her dreams of the perfect wedding, Amelia laughed. "Well, if you want to marry Bennett so soon you're not even going to wear a custom gown, it must really be love!"

Adele signaled for Jeffrey who was grooming the horses by the stable. "Jeffrey! Please bring the carriage around." She looked at Amelia. "I'm going to ride over to Aunt Louisa's to tell her the good news and see if she can help with the dress. Would you like to come?"

"Of course!" She looked at Devon. "Thank you again for this morning. I wouldn't have a chance of making it through this without you."

Devon reached his hand out and fingered the lace lining her shoulder but immediately dropped it back by his side when Adele and Bennett's eyes widened in surprise. "You're welcome," he responded softly.

Amelia climbed up into the carriage after her sister who reached behind her and slammed the door shut, simultaneously hissing, "What was that?"

"It was nothing," Amelia frowned.

"If you say so," Adele said, giggling, but Amelia was too busy watching Devon fade from the view of the carriage window to retort.

Louisa was, of course, thrilled for Adele and happily agreed to alter Juliette's dress. "When I'm through with it, you'll look even prettier than your mother did on her wedding day, and that's saying something!" she stated proudly.

The carriage rolled pleasantly along the road home as the girls contemplated whether or not to serve early season pheasant or seafood as the entrée at the reception.

"Young pheasants can be spectacular when done correctly," Adele stated emphatically.

"Or they can be an utter disaster," Amelia countered. "But it's your wedding Adele, so you should have whatever you want."

The sound of a horse whinnying behind the carriage forced Jeffrey to pull off the road and out of the way of the impatient rider who flew by without acknowledging them.

"What on earth? I wonder what his hurry is about?" Amelia mused. They didn't have to wonder for long, though, because the horse and its rider were galloping away from their house when they arrived home minutes later.

Michael paused at the door where he'd been talking with the stranger and thanked Jeffrey for ferrying the girls across the county and back. Then he stepped closer to Jeffrey and spoke in a hushed voice. He entered the house a bit later as Amelia heard wagon wheels rushing away.

Amelia could stand her curiosity no longer and approached him in his study. "Father, whatever is the matter? Where did Jeffrey rush off to?"

His face was grave. "We've received word from our suppliers along the coast that a hurricane is quickly approaching from the Southeast. The captains of the ships coming in from the sea are saying it's the worst they've ever seen. I sent Jeffrey to Atlanta to get extra building supplies and rations for the mercantile in case it causes damage inland and people need quick access to resources."

The peaceful sunlight tauntingly poured in through the curtains as Amelia looked in the direction of Savannah. It was a hundred miles away, but nevertheless, the thought of a hurricane making landfall in the city, with so many thousands of people living there, brought an unsettling chill to her bones.

Chapter 14

Salty, sea borne squalls pounded against the boarded-up windows of Sullivan's Pine just two days later. Despite the summer temperatures that stubbornly stood firm against the impending rains, Amelia couldn't help but shiver as she pulled her shawl tightly around her when a particularly forceful gust rattled the house.

Juliette busied herself experimenting with hairstyles for Adele on her wedding day. Today's venture was an intricate pattern of small braided buns with white ribbon woven throughout. Adele looked up at Amelia for approval, and Amelia nodded enthusiastically. "Yes, that one is, beyond a doubt, my favorite." She held up a mirror for Adele to see for herself.

Her sister gasped in delight. "Mother, its perfect!"

Juliette smiled in approval. "Then it's settled."

The parlor door flew open, and Louisa, hair tousled wildly from the wind, rushed inside holding a parcel wrapped in a blanket. She set it on Adele's lap.

"Well,? What do you think?" she asked breathlessly?

Adele furiously tugged at the strings until she could unfold the dress. She stood, holding it up in front of herself, and let the train cascade to the floor. "Please, Amelia, help me slide out of my dress and into the gown. I can't wait another minute to try it on!"

Amelia unthreaded the crisscrossed ribbon which held Adele's outer shell in place and lifted the dress up and over Adele's head, careful not to jostle her hair so they could get the full preview of what she would look like on her wedding day. Adele held her arms up for Juliette and Louisa to slide the cap sleeves over her arms. Then Amelia laced up the bodice and bustled up the train so Adele could walk in the dress to ensure it fit correctly.

"Well done, Louisa," Juliette said, smiling.

"Thank you! Oh, and I almost forgot!" Louisa smiled mysteriously as she pulled a small package from her pocket.

Adele carefully opened the package and held up the beautifully embroidered pale blue handkerchief that was inside.

"It's your 'something blue,'" Louisa explained.

"It's beautiful, Aunt Louisa. Thank you!"

"Not nearly as beautiful as you, my love," she replied.

A sudden clap of thunder sounded almost simultaneously with the pelting of hail outside the window. Amelia was entranced as she peered through the crack in the boards and watched the trees outside bend and sway. Weak branches flew off in a frenzy, bombarding the sides of the house like bullets. She knew the storm had likely lost much of its power, having traveled over land the night before. Still, she'd never seen anything like it. She stood there in a daze, almost admiring the power the storm possessed.

Amelia was awakened from her revelry by her sister, nearly naked in only her petticoat, racing past her out the door towards the garden. "Adele!" she yelled, picking up the outer layers of the gown that Adele had left haphazardly on the floor. "Have you lost your mind? What are you doing?"

Adele didn't stop and instead ran out into the rain and through the garden, cutting off lavish amounts of roses with the kitchen shears she'd grabbed on her way out.

When she raced back into the house, Amelia grabbed the flowers from her and handed her a throw she'd retrieved from the hall linen closet. "Oh you can't be serious, Adele. Flowers? Those probably won't even be alive by next weekend. You could have been killed! No flowers are worth that."

"They most certainly are!" Adele said and frowned in rebellion. "What if the storm destroys all of the others? I have to at least try! What's a wedding without flowers?"

Amelia looked down at her sister disapprovingly. "Well it's also tradition to keep your wedding dress in case your daughter wants to wear it, as I know you'll do, but I don't think any sensible girl would want to wear those petticoats now that they're covered in mud."

Adele sauntered down the hall. "Come with me, Millie. I think we can clean it up before it stains."

Juliette and Louisa were discussing centerpiece alternatives in the doorway of the sitting room when the girls rushed past, and Louisa immediately noticed the problem. Knowing just what to do, she ordered Amelia to get some clean, cold water from the kitchen as she followed Adele into the dressing room.

Amelia did as she was told and came back to see that Louisa was carefully blotting at the mud on the satin with the handkerchief she'd given Adele. "I think we can salvage it if we're careful. Amelia, set the water here, dear, and go fetch me another cloth. This one is getting too dirty." Louisa held up the muddy piece of fabric, and Amelia reached out to take it but gasped audibly when she looked down at the small piece of cloth.

Louisa looked up at her quizzically. "Millie, are you all right, dear?"

Amelia nodded, looking towards the window. "I'm fine. It's just the storm." The room had begun to spin, and she felt sweat suddenly dripping down her back. Looking for a quick escape, she turned and flew from the room, clutching the handkerchief, ran down the stairs to the kitchen, and over to the farthest corner of the room. Still clinging to the fabric square with her left hand, Amelia braced herself on the edge of the chopping block, lowered her head towards the ground, and tried to breathe. She was afraid she was going to faint.

"In hindsight, I probably should have given her my garter."

Chapter 15

Louisa's voice echoing over the gale force winds outside made Amelia jump. She turned around and tried to regain her composure. "I'm sorry? I'm not sure what you mean," she managed.

"I've known you an entire lifetime, Amelia," her aunt smirked. "I can tell when you're lying. It was the handkerchief, wasn't it?"

"Aunt Louisa, I really don't—" Amelia began, looking towards the stairs in panic. But Louisa took a quick step towards her and grabbed a knife from the sink in the process. "Louisa, what are you doing?"

"Let's not waste time with formality, dear. I know you detest it."

Desperate, Amelia decided that keeping her aunt talking might give her enough time to get away or at least to scream for help.

"Yes. It was the handkerchief. It's embroidered with your initials."

"Obviously," her aunt mocked. "But I still don't see how that helped you come to the realization that I killed Ethan."

"His business ledger. Your initials were in it."

"That's impossible. I made him swear he would keep our name off the books. I didn't want that bloody Desoto to find out we were involved. Then he'd try to get his grubby hands on our money, too."

Amelia couldn't take her eyes off the knife Louisa was casually shifting from hand to hand, but she kept talking. She had to stall Louisa long enough for someone to notice their absence and come looking. She began slowly inching her way towards the stairs up to the garden since Louisa was blocking the stairwell to the main part of the house. "There was another ledger. A hidden one Ethan kept at the house. Devon found it in his desk. It had everything in it. My father's actual investment and another next to the initials PdS. Or at least what I thought was PdS. But it was really P. O. L. S., wasn't it? The O and L just ran together. Patrick O'Brien and Louisa Sullivan. He tried to keep things coded even in his secret ledger. He tried to keep your name out of it."

She didn't want to move too suddenly, or Louisa would block her path to that exit as well. All it would take was a simple push of the light butcher's block table, and she'd be trapped.

"Well, I do appreciate a man who keeps his word," Louisa said and laughed haughtily.

In spite of the situation, Amelia's nerves bristled. "If he kept his end of whatever deal it was you made, why did you kill him?"

"Because he wouldn't let it go—that stupid railroad. We'd already lost so much money, and the Farmer's Alliance was on the verge of losing its power already." Louisa paused, trying her best to look pitiful. "We're bankrupt, you know."

She hadn't known, and even though her aunt was trying to hold her hostage with a knife, she still felt a twinge of sadness for her. Amelia knew her aunt, or at least she thought she did, and, right or wrong, Louisa's social status was part of who she was. In a way, she could understand how Louisa would become desperate facing bankruptcy. "So you lost your money," Amelia said as she edged closer to the garden stairs. "You lost your money, and you were so angry that you killed him."

"Of course not. I had a plan. *We* had a plan. We were going to partner with your father. It had all been worked out. We would have recovered. But then Ethan just couldn't let it go. When he brought it up that night at dinner, I could see that glint in Patrick's eye. *He* didn't want to let it go either. I knew if Ethan got to Patrick on his own, he'd try to invest again, and then we *would* lose everything."

Pretending to let her aunt's words sink in for a moment, Amelia shifted her weight onto her back foot, readying herself to run up the stairs and outside. But before she did, she wanted answers.

"So it was all about money. You killed the love of my life. My future husband. For money. How could you do that to him? To me? Do you not care about me at all? And then—you came and sat with me, cried with me when he died. How sick are you that you could try to grieve with me when it was your fault he was dead?"

Louisa's face changed for a moment, showing a glimmer of the woman Amelia had once known.

"I *was* sad for you. What happened wasn't intentional. I didn't follow him out to the path planning to kill him. But when I told him to leave Patrick alone, he'd laughed. He said I was just being a silly woman, worrying about something I didn't understand, and the only thing I remember is picking up the closest thing I could find and hitting him with it. I didn't intend for him to die. You need to know that."

Louisa's excuses fell on deaf ears. "What about everything that happened after that? Was Gabriel in on it, too? Did you have someone try to run me and Devon off the road?"

Louisa smirked. "I didn't need someone to do that. I put on Patrick's clothes, and I did it myself. I thought it would scare you into backing down on your investigation. But it didn't. You didn't even slow down when you almost got your mother killed. That's when I knew that you weren't going to stop. And Gabriel Desoto was just a convenient distraction. I thought the sheriff would have enough to arrest him with the evidence of his financial ties to Ethan and in light of his past crimes. But then you threw the suspicion on Bennett." She laughed. "That was even better."

"And now you're going to kill me? Uncle Patrick's not an imbecile, Louisa. He'll figure it out." Amelia took another tiny step towards the door. "What then? You will kill him, too?"

"Darling, I can't see a situation where I let you live, and I don't go to prison. If I go to prison, I lose everything. I can't let that happen, Amelia.

"You're deranged! Have you no soul?"

Amelia saw anger flash across her aunt's face, and Louisa lunged toward her, the knife poised above her head. Amelia knew she had run out of time. She flung her body forward and bolted up the stairs, nearly pushing the door off its hinges as she stumbled into the garden. The roar of the rain was absolutely deafening. She was soaked in seconds, and she knew her heavy dress would slow her down, but she didn't have time to take it off; the best she could do was pick up her skirts and run.

Amelia ran without direction, simply trying to escape. She paused to catch her breath behind the trunk of a thick pine. Rapidly considering her options, Amelia thought about going to the front of the house where she could hopefully pull the bell cord and at least alert them that she was outside, but leaving the cover of the trees would be suicide. Branches and fencing and wrenched tin hurtled through the air, slamming into the house and threatening to break the windows.

She looked around her as she ran deeper into the woods. She could run to the cabin at the edge of the property, but May was there with Baby Ethan. She couldn't risk Louisa harming them trying to get to her. Her only other option was the carriage house. If she could make it there she might be able to get on one of the horses and ride into town. The threat of the storm would remain, but she could reach help more quickly on horseback.

The howl of the wind assaulted her ears as she covered her head in a feeble attempt to protect it from the elements. Amelia's house shoes slid uncontrollably in the mud as she tripped over fallen trees and limbs. At last, she propelled the door open into the carriage house. The horses were all understandably panicked by the storm and snorted in protest as she ran from stall to stall, trying to find her brother's stallion, Faborr, whom she knew she could ride bareback. Mercifully, he was in the third one she checked. Rapidly, she guided him out of the stall by his mane to the mounting stool and throttled her leg up and over his back. Her feet jabbed into his sides, sending him hurtling out into the rain, but the instant the hail hit his face he reared and tried to turn back.

Amelia kicked his flanks again, urging him forward. "Please, Faborr," she begged. "We have to get out of here."

She heard a commotion in the carriage house and turned around to see Louisa mounting her own horse still holding the knife in the sash of her dress.

Amelia forcefully dug in her heels a final time, and at last he obeyed, galloping down the road. She held up her arm in front of her face, trying to shield her eyes from the rain so she could see where she was going, but it was no use. The sheets of water were nearly horizontal, assaulting her like needles as she rode furiously away from the house. Her only hope at this point was to outrun her aunt until she could find someone else foolish enough to be out in the deluge.

But she didn't know this horse, and Louisa had the advantage of being on her stallion, Ranger, and caught up to Amelia within seconds of emerging from the barn. She hollered through the rain, "Just give it up, Amelia! You can't outrun me!"

She was right. *Dear God, please. Help me... Think, Amelia. Where do you have an advantage?* The wind swirled violently around her as rain beat into her face. She swatted the water from her eyes and then she knew. *The river!* If she could get to the river before her aunt, she might be able to swim farther downstream and circle back to the house on foot. She yanked the horse to the right and clung to the horse's mane as they tumbled down the embankment towards the water's edge.

Her aunt didn't hesitate as she followed, yelling, "You're insane if you think you can survive that river during this storm Amelia. Drowning is a terrible way to die!"

Amelia didn't listen. Louisa was stalling. She pulled back on the reins and jumped off, freeing the horse who hobbled up the hill and retreated back towards the house. She glanced back one more time, desperately looking for any other way to escape, and then dove headfirst into the river. She started to take a stroke to break away from the bank, but something caught her skirt. She looked back and laid eyes on Louisa, eyes feral with rage, trying to tug her back. She clawed at Amelia's skirt with the knife, slicing it to shreds. Pain seared through her leg as the knife pierced her thigh. She screamed in agony but knew that focusing on the pain would only slow her down and get her killed. She reached back and tried to knock the knife from Louisa's hand, but Louisa was still holding her ankle, and she couldn't maneuver her body into the right position to reach the knife.

Louisa lashed out with the knife again, this time puncturing Amelia's ribcage. The pain was almost unbearable as she gasped for a breath. Blood steeped with air gurgled into her mouth as she sucked in again. Amelia gaped across the river to the opposite bank. *I'll never out-swim her now. I'll drown first. Can I get across to the other side?* She tried leveraging her foot off the riverbed to lurch away from her aunt and out into the open water, but that required too much breath.

She barely moved an inch. The stab wound made it impossible to take in enough air. Clawing at the water, she willed herself to swim forward, but with Louisa clinging to her leg, Amelia knew she'd never get free.

Louisa hoisted the knife above her head, ready to strike again with what would undoubtedly be the final blow, and Amelia saw her last chance to break free. With her free leg, she kicked as hard as she could, knocking Louisa, who was already off-balance, backward. She let go of Amelia's other leg and tumbled backwards into the water, dropping the knife into the current.

Louisa stood back up in a rage, an evil determination in her eyes, and she dove towards Amelia with outstretched arms, catching her skirt once again. But Amelia, empowered with the knowledge that her aunt's only available weapon now was her bare hands, thought she might stand a chance to slip out of Louisa's reach into the current if she lost some of the weight of her clothes. She dug through the water with one arm, still trying to break free, and pulled at the waistline of her skirt with the other. Finally, she found the button that attached it to her chemise.

The wind and rain had increased the speed of the current to a wash of whitewater and Amelia could feel the strong undertow threatening to drag them both under, but she kept working at the button, furiously kicking her legs, trying to break free from Louisa's determined grasp. At last Amelia felt the button give way. Thrusting her free hand under the water, she pulled off the skirt. She heard Louisa growl in anger when she slipped free of her clenched hand. As Amelia began to swim out into open water, she again heard Louise splashing after her, but before she could look back to see how much distance Louisa had covered, her head collided with something huge and hard, and everything began to spin. A deafening tone echoed in Amelia's ears as she turned her eyes back towards the shore and saw Louisa's red hair slipping below the surface of the water.

Amelia's last conscious thought was to take a breath in case the current pulled her under. Without it, she knew she would not leave the river alive, but before she could will her burning sides to draw in a deep breath, everything went black.

The first thing she saw was a blinding white light, and then she felt searing pain as she spewed water and bile. The pain in her side nearly made her lose consciousness again, and then she realized she was no longer among the thrashing rapids but was on land. What she'd thought were the racing waves spilling over her head were torrents of rain from the hurricane, still ferociously pounding down on the earth. Amelia coughed again and grabbed her side, watching as blood spilled out from between her fingers. She heard the sound of fabric ripping and suddenly remembered Louisa. Terrified, she held up her arms to defend against another blow when a strong arm grabbed her wrist and grasped her hand.

"Amelia! You need to hold still. I have to stop the bleeding."

Squinting through the rain, she recognized the voice and whimpered, "Devon?"

"It's okay, Millie, you're going to be okay. Just hold on until I can get you to a doctor."

She nodded and watched as he pulled his shirt over his head and tore it down the middle. He tied the two pieces together, wrapped the makeshift tourniquet around her ribcage, and tied it tightly. She screamed in agony.

"I know that feels terrible, but I have to put enough pressure on the wound to slow down the bleeding. Do you understand?"

Amelia nodded and then looked frantically back towards the river.

"Louisa…" she managed to say through gritted teeth.

"She's dead," Devon grimaced.

"Are you sure?" she moaned as he tightened the knot on her side further.

"Yes. I saw her go under right before I pulled you up from the edge of the water, and she didn't come back up."

Amelia laid her head back on the soaked earth in relief. She could feel herself slipping out of consciousness again from the pain and the loss of so much blood, but before she did, she managed to ask, "How did you know where to find me?"

He held up the handkerchief. "I came by to check on you all before the storm hit, and Adele said you'd gone to get water for her dress. I found this in the kitchen, saw the monogram and the open door and figured you'd tried to escape to get help. When I saw the carriage house gates open I knew you'd gone for the river. It was your only chance because you wouldn't have been able to outride Louisa. She may have been an expert rider, but I've never seen anyone swim better than you."

Devon stood up and bent over to carefully scoop her off the ground and head for a doctor. The last thing Amelia saw before she closed her eyes from exhaustion was the river, nearly overflowing, rushing furiously away from her and taking the horrors of the past year with it.

Epilogue

The first blooms of the rambunctious orange mums had sprung into flower ahead of their time, making Amelia smile as she poured water from the pitcher and down onto the earth at their roots. The other orange variety she and Adele had planted several years ago always came up right on time in late September, but, for some reason, these orange ones enjoyed making their debut each year in the heat of August, so she clipped the blooms and placed them in the vases she'd brought out from the house. The blossoms had mercifully survived the hurricane and opened just a few days later. They would be perfect for the wedding.

Amelia bent down and pulled up a few small weeds fighting for space in the garden alongside the autumn squash seedlings she'd sowed a few days ago. Uncle Patrick had dropped off some seeds on his way to the coach to head up to his son's home in New York the day after Louisa's funeral. He didn't stay but for a moment, but it was long enough for Amelia to see that although he was a broken man and still quite shell-shocked, he was going to try to press on. The sheriff determined that Patrick had no foreknowledge of Louisa's part in Ethan's death, which relieved the family.

"Harry wants me to come up to New York and help them with their business, and I think I'll be happy there, eventually." He nodded as if trying to convince even himself. A steady flow of tears ran down his ruddy cheeks, and he made no attempt to stop them.

He went inside to find Adele and Bennett, apologizing that he'd be missing the wedding and pleading for their forgiveness for the months Bennett had spent in prison. Bennett was just as gracious with him as he'd been with Amelia.

"Patrick, you've nothing to apologize for. You didn't know. We'll miss you at the wedding, but we understand it would just be too much."

Nodding, Patrick stood and said no more. He returned to the stable to fetch his horse so he could catch the train in Atlanta. Michael Sullivan, who had remained the sturdy rock he always was in spite of the shock and sadness at losing his only sister, stopped Patrick at the stable. He took his hand and shook it, wishing him nothing but happiness, and stood stoically as he watched his brother-in-law ride away for, perhaps, the last time.

Samuel, May, and baby Ethan were in the process of packing up their cottage to move to O'Brian's Plantation and run the farm for Patrick. They would send him a small portion of the proceeds but would keep most of the profit for themselves. Amelia was delighted for them. Samuel had the same passion for the land that Patrick did. He would make an amazing farmer.

Though everyone seemed to have made peace with the tragedies that had befallen them, Amelia still hadn't been able to come to terms with Louisa's death or the fact that it had been she who had killed Ethan. She'd resigned herself to the fact that she might never understand how someone could kill another human being because of money, especially someone with no history of violence.

No one in the family could make sense of it, but her mother had so far come the closest. "Desperate people do desperate things," she'd said the night before the funeral.

Amelia supposed she was right, but she knew the wounds left by Louisa's betrayal, and even her death, would stay with her for the rest of her life. It was a strange thing to mourn someone and yet also feel relieved that the person was gone. But she did feel, finally, as if a burden had been lifted from her shoulders ever since she'd discovered Louisa's guilt. She knew she had done Ethan justice and now felt at peace to move forward.

"Good morning, sunshine!" a cheerful voice greeted her from the patio.

Amelia stood and turned to welcome the visitor, dusting the dirt from her hands. "Good morning to you."

Devon sat down on the garden bench and stretched out his legs. "What a perfect morning for a stroll!"

"Isn't it? Though judging from the mess of my hair, I think it's going to be quite humid and hot as the day progresses. I'll have to take another bath before the ceremony this afternoon." She joined him on the bench. "How was your trip back home?"

"Couldn't have gone any better. They agreed with me that opening a branch office of the firm here to serve Oak County is an excellent idea. I can't believe there aren't any other law firms in the county!"

"You'll certainly be busy! When will you be here permanently?"

I need to find a place to live before anything else. Bennett and Adele have been so kind to invite me to stay at the house while they're away on their honeymoon, but somehow I think I won't be as much of a welcome guest when they return," he said and chuckled.

Amelia thought for a moment. "Why don't you move into the caretaker's cottage here? It will be empty in a week."

"There's an idea," he said, smiling. "That just might work. Bennett has agreed to let me use half of his office for my practice, so that would clear up the only other detail stopping me from relocating."

"Then it's settled! Mother will be so pleased to have someone out there in the cottage, taking care of it, though you may be awakened by a stray cow occasionally—just a fair warning."

"Better than being awakened by a seagull flying into my window."

Laughing, Amelia shook her head. "You're joking."

"I swear. Not a pleasant way to wake, trust me."

"I don't imagine so," Amelia said and laughed.

They stood and walked back towards the house as the sun was heating up the air quickly. When they entered the breakfast room, her parents were drinking their juice and eating poached eggs. Amelia shared her suggestion that Devon move into the cottage after Samuel and May moved to the farm.

"Of course, you're welcome to live here," Juliette smiled. "We're so happy to hear you've decided to stay. That will help Bennett and May immensely as we all try to move forward."

They finished eating quickly, and Amelia gathered a few leftover items on a tray to take up to Adele. She'd said she was too nervous to eat that morning, but Amelia knew the last thing anyone needed was an unconscious bride, so she would ensure she at least drank some juice. She tapped lightly on her sister's door, and Nancy let her in.

The sight she beheld when she stepped into the room was one of the loveliest she could recall. Adele was seated at her dressing table, dabbing rouge on her cheeks, although she really didn't need it. Her face glowed brilliantly with the anticipation of a blissful beginning. Her hair was already up, and the sunlight glinted off the shimmer of her delicate golden chignon, all twisted and entwined.

When Adele saw Amelia in the reflection of the mirror she smiled and stood to greet her. "Well then? What do you think?"

Amelia wrapped her sister in her arms and kissed her cheek. "I've never seen a more glorious bride."

"Thank you." Adele spied the food tray. "I told you I'm too nervous to eat!"

Amelia frowned and poured a glass from the pitcher. "Come now, Bennett needs an energetic bride. He can't carry the crowd we're expecting on his own. He's not that amiable," she teased.

"Ugh. Okay. I'll eat just a tad," Adele replied, nibbling on a biscuit and taking a sip of the juice.

Fixing a strand of hair that threatened to escape the hold of one of the braids, Amelia gazed at her sister who had suddenly seemed to age a lifetime overnight. She wasn't the little girl Amelia had scolded, chided, and protected anymore. Today, she was a woman.

"Are you all right, Millie?"

She smiled. "Yes, I'm fine. I'm just delighted for you and Bennett. I love you both so." Her throat swelled as she choked back tears, and her sister hugged her tightly.

"I love you, too. I'm only sorry that you can't have this, too. You would have been a beautiful bride."

Tears sprung to Adele's eyes, but Amelia shooed them away. "Let's not do this today. And anyway, I haven't lost hope that someday I will be standing there, just as you are. I just won't be preparing to marry the man I thought I would."

"But his name very well may still be Bennigan." Adele giggled in spite of her tears.

Amelia's cheeks grew warm, but she said nothing. Her thoughts and feelings were all jumbled since the revelation of Ethan's cause of death. So much had happened, and so many of her relationships had grown or shifted. But today was not the time to try and sort it all out.

Juliette stepped into the room. "Adele, dear, it is time to put on your dress."

Amelia excused herself and went down the hall to freshen up and get into her own gown.

When she emerged a bit later, Adele and their mother were also coming down the hallway towards the parlor to await the start of the ceremony.

Juliette took an arm of each of her daughters, and they walked slowly down the stairs. "I know I don't say it often enough, but I am so proud of each of you, *ma fifilles*. You have both weathered this past year graciously and have come out better for it. It could have destroyed you"—she looked directly at Amelia as she finished—"but, instead, it has made you stronger."

Amelia started to speak, but her eyes were drawn to the door where Devon was assisting Samuel in greeting the early wedding guests. When his eyes met hers, the warmth she had begun to feel every time he was near her intensified to an almost oppressive heat that made her take in an extra breath of air.

He said nothing as she approached, but his face spoke volumes. Amelia ducked shyly, but she smiled at him, and he in return. Suddenly things didn't seem quite as confusing as they had before. Now there was only peace and promise, and it was glorious.

The ceremony was beautiful and sweet. As everyone knew she would be, Adele was the perfect bride, and Bennett melodramatically breathed an audible sigh of relief when the minister announced that they were now and forevermore Mr. and Mrs. Bennett Bennigan.

Amelia had to admit that Adele had been wise in her choice of the young pheasants as the entrée. They were magnificent. Chef Boudin outdid himself with the oyster appetizers and cream cheese petit fours for dessert in lieu of a cake.

They danced and laughed, and the afternoon passed quickly. Before she knew it, Amelia was kissing Adele and Bennett goodbye as they set off to catch a train in Atlanta for the coast where they would sail to France for a month.

"I love you, Adele. Have a wonderful time," she whispered in her sister's ear.

"I love you more, Millie."

After they had bid the last guests farewell, the remaining Sullivans and Bennigans retired to the drawing room for coffee and tea. They each settled back gratefully onto the comfortable chairs, sipping their drinks, all except Samuel, who played on the floor with the baby. Baby Ethan had behaved like an absolute angel throughout the day.

"Devon, I've been meaning to ask—how does it look along the coast?" Michael queried.

Devon's face grew grim. "It's bad, I'm afraid. The hurricane destroyed most of the homes and businesses within walking distance of the shore and damaged structures many more miles inland."

"That's terrible," Amelia said. "And what about the people? Did many lose their lives?"

He sighed. "They're not sure yet how many, but it's in the hundreds, maybe thousands, from what I hear."

"God bless them," Juliette whispered.

Devon nodded agreement. "It is a mess. That's why I plan to go back in a few days—to see how I can help before I move back here. They're still searching for the missing. The debris from the storm is so vast, it's bound to take months before all of the bodies are recovered. They say the Red Cross is setting up headquarters there to help. I'm going to go there when I return to Savannah and see if I can assist in the efforts."

Standing and straightening her dress, Amelia walked towards the door.

"Millie? Where are you going, girl?" her father inquired.

"To pack my trunk."

CPSIA information can be obtained
at www.ICGtesting.com
Printed in the USA
LVHW081438091118
596563LV00016B/549/P